MW00789918

When the Dog Bites

A Madison Revere Mystery

by

Glen Ebisch

This book is fiction. All characters, events, and organizations portrayed in this novel are the product of the author's imagination or are used fictitiously. Any resemblance to actual persons—living or dead—is entirely coincidental.

Copyright © 2019 by Glen Ebisch

All rights reserved. No parts of this book may be reproduced or transmitted in any form or by any means, electronic or mechanical, including photocopying, recording or by any information storage and retrieval system, without written permission from the author, except for the inclusion of brief quotations in a review.

For information, email Cozy Cat Press, cozycatpress@aol.com or visit our website at: www.cozycatpress.com

COZY CAT
PRESS

ISBN: 978-1-946063-94-6
Printed in the United States of America

10 9 8 7 6 5 4 3 2 1

To Maureen

Chapter 1

It was on a cool evening in early October that I first realized how unstable Otto really was. Oh sure, he'd always been a drama queen. Whenever he wanted something he really wanted it, and he could be insistent almost to the point of becoming aggressive. But that night was the first time I'd personally known him to bite.

My friend Cindy was on a long weekend in Vermont with her on again, off-again fiancé, Myles, and had left me in charge of Otto, who, true to his terrier ancestors, was rooting around my tiny apartment as if every corner were hiding small mammals ripe for the taking. Finally, it reached the point where I could no longer focus on the work I was attempting to do on my laptop. Hoping exercise would relax him into a milder frenzy and simultaneously get his nightly business out of the way, I attached the leash to his collar and took him out for a walk.

We had just reached the street in front of the Victorian house, whose third floor was divided into Cindy's apartment and my own, and had turned to walk toward the pedestrian mall that made up the center of town, when a man in a hurry walked up behind us. I was hardly aware he was there until Otto snarled menacingly and with a quick leap attached himself to the man's lower leg. The man gave a grunt of surprise––shock actually––and frantically but fruitlessly attempted to shake his leg free from the small dog's vice-like jaws.

I reached down and grabbed Otto's collar and attempted to pull him off his victim. This seemed only to increase the growling that came from the center of his small, muscular body, and he continued to hang on with the same fervor he demonstrated with his favorite chew toy. I guessed that to his mind this was all a great game. From the grunts of pain the man was giving, I didn't think he shared that view. Finally, I remembered that I still had a liver-flavored treat in my coat pocket from our earlier walk. I pulled it out and held it in front of Otto's face. At first there was no response; then I shoved it right under his nose. Suddenly—quicker than I could see—Otto let go of the leg and snatched the treat from my fingers. He must have decided that the liver was a more desirable body part than a leg. I quickly pulled on the leash, managing to put several feet of distance between the man and us.

After checking to see that I still had both fingers, I looked over at the victim, who had his pants leg up and was checking out his injuries.

"Are you badly hurt?" I asked in a tremulous voice. I was already filled with guilt that I hadn't kept Otto under better control.

"I'm sure I'll be okay," he said, a shade doubtfully.

Otto gave a sharp pull on the leash as if disappointed to hear that he had not done more damage.

I could see the puncture marks on the man's leg a few inches above the ankle. A couple of lines of blood were oozing down into his sock. "I'm very sorry that happened," I said, feeling my eyes fill with tears.

The man must have heard the emotion in my voice because he looked over at me and smiled. "Don't worry; it's only a dog bite. There's no harm done as long as he's had his shots."

I cleared my throat. "Well, actually he's not my dog. He belongs to my friend Cindy. I'm just the dog sitter."

A concerned expression appeared on his face. "Could you contact your friend and find out about his inoculations?"

I paused, not sure I wanted to disturb Cindy during her romantic rendezvous.

"Could you do it right now?" the man said with some urgency, as if he could feel the rabies starting to course through his veins.

I took a good look at him. He was around six feet tall and slim. I guessed he was a couple of years older than myself, around thirty. I thought most women would consider him passably handsome. I wasn't sure. I tended to judge people by how they acted.

I decided to take a chance.

"Why don't we go upstairs to my apartment? It's right here in this building. I'll call my friend Cindy and find out about the shots. I'll also put some antiseptic on those wounds."

He looked over at Otto a bit doubtfully.

"I'll secure him in his cage. That calms him down."

Indicating that he should stay several steps behind me, I went up the stairs with Otto in the lead. Once we got into the apartment, I picked Otto up, and, before he could gather his strength to object, I shoved him into his crate. Within a few seconds he slumped down on the floor and glared at me silently, as if telling me that I'd be sorry without his protection.

"Okay, you can come in now," I called over my shoulder.

The man slowly came into my apartment as if sure he was walking into an ambush. Once he saw that Otto was behind bars, he visibly relaxed. I decided that introductions were in order.

I stuck out my hand. "I'm Madison Revere, most people call me Madison," I said, heading off any tendency to call me Maddy.

He took my hand in his much larger one. I noticed that his fingers were long and tapered with no wedding ring. "I'm Luke Manning."

I nodded and smiled. He tried to smile as well, but his mouth twitched a little, which I figured indicated that his gnawed on leg might be bothering him. That reminded me.

"Let me call Cindy."

He nodded vigorously.

I went in my bedroom, closed the door, and made my call.

"Hello," an irritable voice answered that I recognized as Cindy's.

"I hope I'm not disturbing anything important," I said cautiously.

"Not unless you consider having a fight important," she replied.

Cindy and her boyfriend seemed to fight as much as they did whatever else they did.

"It's about Otto," I said.

"Oh my God!" she shrieked. "He ran out in traffic and got hit by a car. He's dead!"

"Otto is fine," I assured her. "But he bit someone."

"Otto doesn't bite," Cindy said in a steely voice.

"I saw the holes in the man's leg and watched Otto do it."

"You must be wrong. He's never done it before."

"What about the Jehovah's Witness he bit last year?"

"He shoved a pamphlet at me in an assertive way, and Otto thought I was being threatened."

"And the cable man the year before that?"

"He stepped into my apartment too quickly and Otto thought I was being attacked. Are you sure this man wasn't trying to molest you?"

I thought back. "I didn't really notice him until Otto started chewing on his leg."

"He's probably a rapist or a mugger, and Otto saved your life."

I considered that. "He seems innocent enough."

"Where is he now?"

"In my apartment."

"You let a strange man who tried to attack you into your apartment!"

"I couldn't send him away. He wants to know if Otto has had his shots."

"Of course he has. But who knows what disease this man might have given my poor dog? You should get this guy out of your apartment as soon as possible."

"I'm going to bandage his leg first."

"Why in the world would you do that?"

"Would you like to be sued?"

"No. Of course not."

"Well, as a lawyer, I can assure you that lots of people who get bitten by dogs successfully sue, and it can be a nightmare for the owner. So I think we had better keep this guy as happy as possible. I'll convey your deepest apologies, and do what I can to alleviate his pain."

Cindy grunted. "If you're dead when I get home, do you at least have a name that I can give the authorities."

"His name is Luke Manning."

"Sounds like an alias," she said in a surly tone.

"I'll do what I can to prevent him from suing."

"Thanks," Cindy said grudgingly and hung up.

I put on a bright smile and returned to the living room. Luke was sitting on the sofa examining his leg.

"Good news," I said happily, as if announcing the end of a worldwide conflict. "Otto has had all his shots. Cindy sends her sincerest apologies."

"Great," he said, getting to his feet. "I guess I'll be going then."

""No," I said louder than I intended. "You have to let me put something on your leg."

"That really isn't necessary. I'll be fine," he said with a grin. "I have to go."

"Really, we should do something. All that talk you hear about a dog's mouth being cleaner than a human's is nonsense. You can get all sorts of infections from a dog bite."

He settled back down on the sofa, looking worried all over again.

"Let me see what I have in the medicine chest," I said. I went into the bathroom and surveyed my supplies. If he had an itch in his feminine areas, I was well supplied, but all I could find for cuts and abrasions was an out of date spray can of something I'd used for poison ivy several years ago. Better than nothing, I thought, returning to the living room.

"Pull up your pants leg please," I said, trying to sound my most nurse-like. He obliged. "This may sting a little," I said, immediately spraying a large amount on each side of his leg.

He jerked and writhed as if demons were leaving his body.

"That stuff sure is powerful," he gasped a few seconds later.

"It should do the trick. Now let me get something to cover that wound."

I went in my bedroom and returned with a white cotton handkerchief. Then I went into the kitchen and poked around in the utility drawer. I came back and settled down next to him. I had to admit that he had a rather shapely calf, hardly hairy at all.

"Is that a handkerchief?" he asked.

"Afraid I'm out of gauze, but it's clean," I replied spreading it over his leg, so it covered both sides. Then I pulled a good length of tape off the role.

"Is that duct tape?" he asked.

I nodded. "Afraid I'm out of adhesive as well, but this should work even better." I wrapped a long length of the gray tape around his leg and made sure it was secure. Then I sat back and admired my handiwork. His leg looked pretty good if you ignored the fact that it somewhat resembled a hot water pipe that had just been repaired. "All done," I said brightly. "Now that wasn't so bad, was it?"

He stared at me. "You aren't a nurse, are you?" he asked, as if ready to swear off the entire medical profession if I said I was.

"Nope, I'm a lawyer."

He broke into a hearty laugh. I found myself thinking that he might be a fun person to be around.

"You didn't have to do all this. I never intended to sue."

I blushed. "One can never be too sure."

He took my right hand and held it for a moment. "Well, thank you for all the attention. Now I feel that I owe you. Would you be interested in having dinner with me tomorrow?"

"Oh, you don't have to do that. I was just following a humanitarian urge."

He smiled as if I'd said something funny. "Actually, I think you have an obligation to have dinner with me tomorrow. As my caregiver, you have to check on your patient. I could develop a raging infection between now and tomorrow night. You'd want to know, wouldn't you?"

He had a point. I gave him my phone number, and he tapped it into his phone. "Please call me any time if you don't feel well tonight or tomorrow," I said.

"If you don't hear from me, why don't we meet at the Shore Side Inn," he said, naming a restaurant several blocks away. "I could pick you up here."

"No need, I'll meet you there," I said quickly. Tonight had been an exception, but normally, on the rare occasions when I dated, I preferred to meet a man on neutral ground.

"Thanks again, Madison." He began to walk with a severe limp. "Only kidding," he said smiling, when I gasped with concern. He walked the rest of the way to the door quite normally, but I had a feeling he was being stoical. "See you tomorrow."

I nodded and closed the door behind him. I looked over at Otto, who was staring at me from between the bars as if he were the victim of a biased jurisprudence system. I let him out of the cage, and he proceeded to run wildly around the room.

I'd heard of men borrowing their friends' dogs in order to meet women. I think the reasoning was that women took a pet to be a sign that a man would be responsible with a child. I wondered what a man would think of a woman with a vicious dog. Maybe he'd think she was exciting.

Just shows how wrong you can be.

Chapter 2

I got to the office early the next morning and sat at my desk daydreaming about my upcoming date. I work at Baker, Kerr, and Finch, a small law firm in Shore Side, New Jersey, a cute resort town I ended up in because my parents used to take us there for summer vacations from the Philadelphia area where we lived. I'd gone to law school in New Jersey, so I thought it easiest to take the bar exam in that state, since I had no desire to live near my parents. Not knowing where to live in New Jersey once I passed the bar, I chose the path of least resistance and returned to a place that I had visited.

I'd worked at Baker and Kerr for two and a half years, which meant that in another six months I'd either be promoted to associate partner or let go. So it was a stressful time for me. Mostly I handled wills, real estate transactions, and the occasional small business contract. I never got near anything involving litigation, which was fine by me. Conflict, in my opinion, was always something to be avoided. Whether this peaceable attitude would prevent me from becoming an associate was hard to know.

The three men who had their name on the door were each rather different. Baker was in his seventies and pretty much retired. He came in to greet the occasional special client, but was generally absent. When our paths did cross, he was grandfatherly, cordially asking me—without saying my name, which he probably didn't remember—how I was getting along. He was nice, but I doubted he was much involved in promotion decisions. Kerr was a good ten years younger and the captain of the ship. He was dynamic, with a military bearing and a short haircut to match. He had a staff of his own on the other side of the building, so we rarely came into contact. I suspected he liked the fact that I was a hard worker, but was not so keen on the fact that I wasn't out making contacts to generate more business. What they don't teach you in law school is that an awful lot of the legal business is a matter of mixing in the community in order to generate clients. Being a bit of a recluse, I was pretty useless at meeting new people, although I did once have a client in a nursing home and by doing their hair managed to win over a couple of her friends to have me do their wills.

That leaves the third partner, Haldon Finch. Sounds like a type of rare bird, doesn't it? As in "Joe, isn't that a Haldon Finch?" And indeed, he is a rare bird, with blond hair that perpetually stands on end, and a never fully satisfied desire to make my life miserable. As far as I know, I've never done anything to insult him, so it must be one of those cases of hate at first sight because he has tormented me since I sat down behind my desk. He has a small staff consisting of Sherri Martin, his legal secretary, Phil Cleary, who last year became an associate, and myself. You'd think I'd at least outrank the secretary, but you'd be wrong. A stylish woman in her forties, she's been with Finch for almost twenty years, and is higher in the pecking order than Phil or myself.

Being at the bottom, I get all the dirty work.

"Why isn't there any coffee made?" Finch shouted from the outside office.

Oops! I'd been so involved in my own proto-romance that I'd forgotten my most significant chore as a lawyer, being a waitress. I rushed into the outer office. Sherri sat behind her desk, ten feet from the coffeemaker. She could have warned me that I had forgotten the coffee. Indeed, she could have made it herself, not that she ever would. Instead, she gave me one of her patented aloof looks as I ran out to where Finch stood, turning red with rage.

"Revere, you have only one essential job to perform around here, and that's to make the morning coffee. If you can't do that much, you may as well stay home."

"Yes, sir," I said grimly, biting back a fiery retort. I knew he could fire me—supporting it with some bogus claim about my legal incompetence—and neither Baker nor Kerr would bat an eye. The firm received a blizzard of resumes from those seeking a position every week as law schools continued to churn out more and more graduates for fewer and fewer jobs. I wasn't a victim of gender discrimination so much as a victim of supply and demand.

"Well, get on with it, I have a client coming in by half past, and I *need* my caffeine."

Having made his wishes known, Finch turned on his heel and marched back to his office. I fiddled around with the coffee machine, and by the time I was settled back behind my desk again, the beautiful smell of fresh coffee was filling the suite of offices. I went back to working on a will for a young couple that had come in last week. It was pretty standard stuff, so my mind had half drifted to dinner tonight. I wondered what Luke did for a living, whether he had ever been married, whether he had . . .

I suddenly became aware that there was a shadow in my office. I looked up and Haldon Finch stood there with a complexion, which, if it got any ruddier, would result in a disabling loss of blood flow to the brain. I gave him a quizzical look.

"I think you know by now, Ms. Revere, that you not only make the coffee, but you bring a cup to my office. Not tomorrow, but today."

"Yes, sir," I said, starting to get up.

"Sit down," he barked.

I dropped back down and noticed for the first time that he had a thick file in his right hand. He raised the folder three feet above the surface of my desk and let it drop. It hit the surface like an elevator whose main cable has snapped. Startled, I rolled my chair backwards until I hit the file cabinet behind me. Given the small size of my windowless office, that wasn't very far. Notes, pens, and pencils flew off the desk top onto the floor. Finch's face creased into one of his rare smiles at the chaos he had caused.

"What's that?" I mumbled.

"That, Ms. Revere, is the Mercer file. Are you familiar with the name Mercer?"

I nodded. "Edna Mercer. She died recently and you're settling her estate."

"Precisely. But more to the point, you are helping me settle her estate. All the information you need is contained in this file. I want to see the completed documents on my desk, ready for my signature, by the end of next week."

"But ... "

"But what?"

"I thought Phil handled the Mercer file."

"Phil has other things to do, and it's about time you took more responsibility. You'll be coming up for review soon, and quite frankly your prospects aren't looking very good. You have to prove something to me, Revere, so you'd better do a good job on this."

I was tempted to make a face at his back as he left the room, but was glad I hadn't when he suddenly looked back over his shoulder.

"And get me my coffee," he ordered.

After I'd gotten Finch his coffee—which for the record he didn't thank me for—and put the things back on my desk, I lifted up the Mercer file which had to be ten inches thick and placed it on top of the file cabinet behind me. It might be a priority for Finch, but the will I was working on had been promised to that young couple in two days. That was my first order of business. Edna Mercer was dead and gone; her heirs would be incredibly rich soon enough.

Two hours later, I was satisfied with the draft of the will I had completed, and decided that it was time I got to the bottom of why I was handling the Mercer estate rather than Phil. Although Finch had always been the smiling glad hander when Edna came in to make changes in her will or trust, for all the time I'd been here, it was always Phil who did the actual work. Why wasn't he the one to take the estate down the home stretch, so to speak?

I went across the outside office to Phil's office, which was only marginally bigger than mine, but had a narrow window of the sort medieval archers could fire an arrow through. The door was closed, so I knocked. I received a mumbled reply, and I opened the door and peeked inside. Phil had his jacket draped over his chair and was in his shirtsleeves poking through a pile of papers.

"Do you have a minute?" I asked

Although he seemed a bit frazzled, he managed to muster a smile and pointed to the spare chair.

"You're looking particularly nice today," he volunteered.

I stared. I was dressed in my usual work uniform of a dark waist-length jacket, dark skirt, and white blouse. The outfit only varied among a navy, black, or gray skirt with an occasional light pink or light blue blouse.

Sometime I felt like a nun in a little known legal order. If Phil was being honest, and I did look exceptionally good, it had to be due to my excitement at my pending date. I smiled and thanked him. I knew he wasn't coming on to me. We had been friends since I joined the firm, but never anything more than that. The chemistry just wasn't there.

"What can I do for you?" he asked.

"Finch just dropped the Mercer file on my desk— literally. I asked him why you weren't handling it, and he gave me some nonsense about my having to take more responsibility. I was wondering what the truth is."

Phil sighed and looked across the room.

"The truth is I screwed up the Norton contract. Finch discovered it when the folks buying Norton's company gave him a call, and wanted to know why the terms of the contract had been changed."

"Finch hadn't checked it over himself?"

"You know how lazy the man can be. He just wants to sit on the boards of charities and corporations and pretend to be a big man in town." Phil frowned. "But that doesn't excuse the fact that it was my mistake. I've had things on my mind lately."

I waited for him to go on, but he stayed silent.

"So Finch took the Mercer business away from you as punishment?"

"That's right. But, of course, he wouldn't take the trouble to go through all that paperwork himself, so he dumped it on you. Although to be fair, it does give you an opportunity to show what you can do. Edna Mercer was an important client. Even Kerr will notice if you do a good job."

"It appears to be a pretty daunting project."

Phil smiled at me. "Don't worry, I've been handling her stuff for years and know all the ins and outs. If you need any help, come to me. Just don't let Finch catch you."

I nodded my thanks, but immediately determined that I would do it all myself. This was going to be a test for myself of whether I had a real future as an attorney. I enjoyed working with the law. It had structure, which I liked, with occasional room for interpretation, which I enjoyed as well. I also had a good head for numbers, a real advantage when dealing with taxes. But I sometimes wondered if I was good enough to ever make it to senior partner, and I didn't want to remain in a profession where I'd always occupy the second rung.

My parents had raised my two siblings and, to a lesser degree, myself to be winners. Lead sled dogs, who wouldn't spend their whole lives looking at someone else's butt, as my father liked to say. Although I had nodded agreeably when fed the party line, I'd never been convinced that my future truly extended beyond following someone else's tail. I think my parents harbored the same doubts, but were reluctant to express them, at least when I was young.

If I could sort through something as complicated as the Mercer estate, I would have proven to myself that I was in the right career, one where my vision could reach to the distant horizon.

I returned to my desk and began to dig into the Mercer file like a gold miner who has just discovered a new vein of ore. I ate my lunch at my desk, and hardly looked at the clock until it reached five. At that point, I secured the file in my desk, carefully locking it as I did every day. I knew Phil usually left his work out on his desk, which he never locked anyway, and Finch had every surface in his office covered with confidential files, as if this was proof of how productive he was. I, on the other hand, took security seriously. I also cleared off my desktop every night, proving I was neat if not incredibly busy.

I was so into the Mercer file that I might have stayed longer, but I needed time to prepare for my date. I went out to the main office after closing and locking the door to my office. Sherri was gone for the day as was Phil, but it was my misfortune that Finch heard my door close and marched into the outer office to see who was leaving.

"Where are you going, Revere?" he demanded, as if I were a slave trying to escape from the plantation.

"Home," I said softly. Finch usually took two-hour lunches, but stayed late to check on who was leaving when.

"You do realize that there is an urgent need to settle the Mercer estate?"

"Of course. It will be completed by the end of next week as you requested." I might have to work twenty-four hour days from now on to achieve that, but tonight was mine.

"And why must you leave so early? Do you have a *date*?" He gave a quick snort as if that was about as likely as my going on a trip to Mars.

I wasn't about to share anything with him about my personal life, even if it would have given me momentary satisfaction. "I have a friend who is in the hospital and wants me to bring her a few things."

He raised an eyebrow in an exaggerated expression of doubt. I wasn't sure whether he was uncertain as to whether I had any friends or of my willingness to do anything for them. As always when lying, I gave him a bland stare and didn't elaborate.

He pointed an accusing finger at me. "Remember, Revere, you future is hanging on how well you do this project. I can be a loyal friend, but a ruthless enemy."

I gave a half-nod to show that I believed the second part, even if I had serious doubts about the first. Then I turned and left the office.

Chapter 3

Once home, I showered, plucked, and anointed myself until I felt like a sacrificial offering. I looked at my body in the full-length mirror. I occasionally like to do a careful evaluation to update my mental body image. I am about five-five in my bare feet and slender, verging on thin. I believe that when I get old I will simply become thinner and thinner until I dissolve and blow away in the wind. My hair is reddish brown, my hips are narrow, and my breasts are small but pert, at least according to a paramour from law school.

On our first date, he said I had French breasts. I asked what that meant, and he said one of them would fit in an old-fashioned wide-mouthed champagne glass like you see in the black-and-white movies. When I expressed doubt, we adjourned to his apartment in the interest of science where he proved, with some pushing and prodding, that it was true. One thing, of course, led to another, and afterwards I wondered why a guy in his twenties had an old champagne glass around unless he used it as a seduction technique. I hoped he at least washed it occasionally, but you never know with men.

When I told this story to Cindy, she had laughed and said that it would have required at least a medium-sized mixing bowl to try the trick on her. This was true, as she is much more amply endowed than I am, which I've noticed attracts a lot of male attention and is probably nice for Myles, when they're not fighting. But I frequently wonder which of us will be happier with her body in thirty years' time.

I turned away from the mirror and slowly got dressed. I don't own a lot of casual clothes. Aside from my office uniforms, I usually wear jeans and oversized shirts. My mother once told me that was a good look for me because it made me appear waif-like, which might attract a warm-hearted man. I figured it would be more likely to appeal to a man looking for a kitten or a puppy. And no matter how waif-like I looked, my personality inclined toward the stubborn rather than the malleable.

Thinking jeans were too casual for a first date at a nice restaurant; I put on one of my few non-work blouses and a pair of black slacks that accentuated my rather long—for a basically short person—legs. Unlike many shorter women, I chose not to augment my height with high heels, which are dangerous and unhealthy for the feet. Instead, I slipped into a pair of black wedges.

I let Otto out of his crate, and we took a brief walk up and down the block. Once inside, I gave him the run of the apartment. Wearing black, there was no way I was going to carry him to his crate because I'd come away looking like I groomed animals for a living. A worthwhile profession I'm sure, but not the image that I was trying to project.

Finally ready to leave, I said farewell to Otto, who gave me such a soulful look of abandonment, that I promised I'd give him a treat upon my return. I then headed out on my eight-block walk. I could have taken my car, of course, but, as with most old Victorian resort towns, Shore Side has rather inadequate parking, so I could easily end up several blocks from the restaurant. And when I came home, an alert neighbor would, no doubt, have stolen the parking space near the front of my apartment that I had plotted and planned to get for several weeks. All things considered it was easier to walk. I slipped into a dark jacket and headed out into the cool autumn night.

I walked the two blocks to the pedestrian mall, then down its length to the street leading to the restaurant. It felt good to be out, striding along, feeling my muscles strengthen and my lungs taking in the ocean-scented air. As I left the area of the mall, the street became darker and more treacherous, since the old sidewalks were made of slate, which had been pushed up over the years by the freeze and thaw cycle until they stood at high angles as if purposely designed to trip you, I was picking my way along carefully when I heard the rapid footsteps of someone running up behind me.

I turned and saw a dark figure approaching from about twenty feet away. The figure was running directly toward me. This presented me with one of those socially awkward situations. What if the person was in a hurry to keep a dinner reservation and planning to divert around me at the last minute? If I screamed or jumped wildly out of the way, I would appear to be a coward or an alarmist. But if I stood still, would I simply be run over? I chose to stand right under the streetlight where I could be easily seen, and face the individual as he or she approached. The person was about ten feet away when his foot must have caught on one of the slate edges. He flew forward and fell hard on the sidewalk, almost at my feet. In the light from the streetlamp, I could see that he was wearing black clothes topped off with a ski mask.

This was suspicious enough to cause me to instantly turn and run. Since he was probably stunned by his fall, I had a good head start, and even in my dressier shoes, I am a formidable runner. My parents had insisted that each of us children participate in a sport. This, they claimed, had many benefits. It was in the interest of maintaining good health, led to the development of a competitive instinct, and served as something to put on our applications for college. My brother was a much acclaimed football linebacker, my sister a highly aggressive lacrosse player, and I ran cross-country.

I had chosen that activity because it required the least amount of teamwork. There may be no "I" in team, but there is no "team" in cross-country. Each person works on their own, and is aiming to beat not only the other school but also their own teammates. Running alone over the heather and bracken gave me moments of serenity and composure that I have not enjoyed at any other time. Even now, whenever the stresses of the day are getting to me, I close my eyes and imagine the muffled beat of my footsteps heading across a broken field and feel the tensions drift away. I still try to get out a couple of times a week to run in the sand along the ocean.

All of this is to say that I was confident that unless he was an Olympic class runner, I could easily outdistance the person following me to the front door of the Shore Side Inn. I was confident enough that I even stopped once to look back to see if he was coming along behind me, but neither saw nor heard anything. Nonetheless, I kept up a good pace until I was inside the lobby of the restaurant.

Perhaps I was a bit red in the face or looked slightly disheveled because the young woman at the hostess station gave me a suspicious glance.

"Do you have a reservation?" she asked sharply, suddenly alert to her job of keeping out riffraff, even of the more athletic kind.

"I'm here to meet Luke Manning," I said, making it sound more like a business meeting than a date.

The woman scanned the list. "We do have a reservation for a Manning," she said, doubtfully, as if I might be engaged in some kind of elaborate scam to get a table with plans of disappearing without paying.

I'm not sure how our conversation would have progressed, but I suspect it wouldn't have been pretty. But just then a voice behind me softly said, "Madison."

I turned and Luke stood there dressed all in black, and breathing heavily.

"Sorry, I'm late," he said, patting my arm. "I got tied up at work."

I am not by nature a suspicious person, but I will admit that I mentally placed a ski mask over his face and tried to determine if he could be my stalker.

"Is anything wrong?" he asked when I stared and said nothing.

"Not at all," I replied, looking over his clothes for signs of a recent tumble. He appeared spotless. Would the average stalker carry a clothes brush around with him? I doubted it. Still, I wasn't completely convinced of his innocence. However, I also wasn't ready to cancel my date based on such shaky suspicions.

"Why don't we go in to eat?" I said.

"You look very lovely tonight."

I thought I probably looked as if I had just run a hundred yard sprint, but I smiled to express my appreciation of his gallantry.

He smiled as well and walked close beside me as we followed the hostess into the dining room. She led us to a table that would doubtlessly have offered a beautiful view in the daytime of their side garden, but at night it looked out on intimidating darkness. I took a deep breath and sat down. I half expected a leering face to pop up in the window at any moment, and I edged my chair back at bit.

"Are you sure you're okay?" Luke asked.

I nodded and made a few routine comments about the marvelous décor to hide my unease. As one of the classier restaurants in Shore Side, I knew Luke would want me to show my appreciation. When the waitress came around I ordered a glass of white wine and Luke asked for a beer. We spent some time studying the sizeable menu. In the past, I had only eaten at the Shore Side Inn for business luncheons when I paid no attention to the prices, and I was stunned to see what they charged for their entrees.

"Of course, you realize I'll pay for my own meal," I said, as if it were a foregone conclusion. "After all, it's not right that you pay when it was my friend's dog that bit you."

Although I thought he had gone a bit pale as he studied the menu, he rallied valiantly.

"Don't be silly," he said. "I invited you to dinner."

"And it was very kind of you. But perhaps we could go Dutch tonight, and the next time—if there is a next time—we'll work out in advance who is going to pay."

"Well, if you insist," he said reluctantly, but I thought I detected a sigh of relief.

"Speaking of the dog bite," I continued, "how is your leg feeling?"

"Actually, I went to one of those urgent care centers today to have it checked out. Not that I had any reservations about your treatment," he said quickly, "but I just wanted to be certain that I wasn't going to get an infection. They said it looked fine, but insisted I have a tetanus shot just to be on the safe side."

"That was probably wise."

"They thought your bandaging technique was . . . um . . . very original."

"Necessity often makes us inventive."

He nodded and smiled. He reached in his pocket and handed me a white handkerchief. "I laundered it today, so I could return it to you."

"That's very kind of you. Those handkerchiefs are one of my little indulgences. I'm happy to have it back."

"I could tell it was of good quality."

The waitress came back and we placed our orders, each of us choosing something from the lower priced end of the menu. I was pleased to see that he wasn't the sort of man to select one of the most expensive offerings just to impress me.

"You mentioned that you're a lawyer," he said, after the waitress had left. "What type of law do you specialize in?"

"If I were a doctor, you would call me a general practitioner. I handle all of the less demanding aspects of law: real estate, wills, simple contracts, the occasional customer complaint."

"Nothing criminal?"

I shook my head. "People often assume that if you're a lawyer, you're another Perry Mason. That's like thinking all doctors are brain surgeons. Our firm doesn't do criminal law; we refer that out to a practice that specializes in it. We do some civil litigation: insurance claims and accidents. But I don't litigate, I try to avoid conflict."

Luke grinned. "And here I thought all lawyers were aggressive and adversarial."

"Some are. They're the pit bulls of the profession, although I may be maligning pit bulls."

"Let's just say they're the Ottos of the profession," Luke said with a grin.

I frowned. "That may not be quite fair to Otto. He almost never bites unless he thinks his person is threatened."

Luke turned serious. "Did you feel threatened by me the other night?"

I studied him carefully to see if he was gaming me, hiding the fact that he had tried to attack me not once, but twice. But he seemed sincerely concerned.

"No, I didn't," I admitted. "But Otto may have interpreted it that way."

"As long as you didn't."

"I didn't have a chance to be afraid. I'd hardly seen you before Otto attacked."

"He's a good friend to have around."

We paused for a moment as the waitress brought us our salads. After a few moments spend focusing on our food, and commenting on how good it was, I decided it was time for me to hold up my side of the conversation.

"What kind of work do you do?"

He paused for a moment and blushed, as if I'd made an indecent proposal on our first date.

"Actually, I'm an expert . . . an IT expert."

"You know I've been having some trouble with my spread sheet software . . . "

"I deal in software for graphic designs . . . uh . . . it's rather specialized." He filled his mouth with food and began to vigorously chew.

"Is there much call for that in this area?" I asked, when he finished chewing.

"Most of my clients are in Philadelphia."

"That's a pretty long daily commute."

"I can do lots of my work from home, but sometimes I have to go into the city and stay for a couple of days. My schedule is rather erratic."

I opened my mouth to ask another question about his work, but he cut me off.

"It's really technical stuff, only interesting to people in the field. But I bet you meet a lot of different characters in your line."

Half an hour later, I realized that I had talked constantly about work and the folks I had met there.

Our entrée had come and been consumed, and I was still going on about life at the office. Such chattering really isn't like me, and I became aware of the fact that Luke was a really good listener. He maintained eye contact and knew when to ask just the right question to stimulate the further flow of conversation. These weren't skills that most of the men I had dated possessed. With them, if you paused a microsecond for a breath, they interrupted you with what they thought was a fascinating anecdote of their own, which often went on interminably.

As we left the restaurant, Luke offered to walk me home—insisted actually—citing the dangers for a woman alone at night. Although normally I would have objected that Shore Side was hardly a hotbed of crime, after my near assault on the way to the restaurant, I was feeling vulnerable enough to accept his offer. During our walk, I somehow found myself telling stories about when my family used to come to Shore Side for the summer, and how much the town had changed, while still remaining essentially the same.

The only awkward moment came when we reached my front door. I was tempted to invite him in, but I have a sort of informal rule not to do that on a first date.

"I'd invite you up, but Otto currently has the run of the apartment."

Luke laughed. "One encounter with Otto was enough."

"Do you have far to go to get home?" I asked, realizing I'd never inquired where he lived.

"I'm over in West Shore Side," he said, naming a town several miles to the west, which was less pricey because of its distance from the ocean.

"You aren't going to walk there?" I said, shocked.

He smiled. "I'm not that rugged. I have a car parked in the downtown. I just have to walk four or five blocks, and I'll drive from there."

"I had a very good time," I said.

He nodded, and before I could stretch my hand forward for a shake, he leaned toward me and gently kissed me on the lips. Since there was nothing presumptuous about it, I didn't object.

"I might be away on business for a couple of days, but I'll call you as soon as I'm back if you'd be willing to go out with me again."

I nodded. "And remember, next time is my treat."

"We'll see," he replied, as he turned and walked away, looking back once to wave.

I went up the stairs to my apartment, and when I opened the door, Otto came to greet me with surprise and enthusiasm, as if he'd been certain I was dead in a ditch somewhere. After he smelled me for several seconds, he gave me the evil eye, perhaps because he had caught Luke's scent.

"I don't care what you think," I told him. "Luke is a nice guy."

I put his leash on, and we went downstairs for our nightly walk. As we stood there in the cool dark of the night, I hoped that what I had said was true.

Chapter 4

When I got to work the next morning, despite thinking frequently about Luke, I immediately made coffee. The last thing I needed was having Finch spoil my good mood. The man was a constant source of misery, but because he held my professional fate in his hands, I had to be careful in expressing my displeasure. I have a tendency to hold my feeling in until I suddenly snap with a poorly timed explosion of righteous outrage, but I had to keep my feeling tamped down for at least another six months, until I was an associate.

I was just about to dive back into the depths of the Mercer file when Reggie appeared in my doorway. Reggie Shea is an associate who mostly works for Kerr at the other end of the hall. We talk occasionally because we are around the same age and we're both runners. Unlike me, she looked like a runner with a long rangy body and not an ounce of fat to spare.

"I ran the Shoreline Marathon last weekend," she announced proudly.

"How was it?" I'd never run a marathon. I don't like pounding along on city streets and twenty-six miles is more grueling than the three miles or so I'm accustomed to doing from cross-country. I run for pleasure, not to test my endurance. For that I have Finch.

"Great. It was a nice cool day, and I beat my personal best."

"Congratulations."

She nodded. "You should try a marathon. There's one coming up in central Jersey in late November. The Chase the Turkey Run or something like that."

"That's not much time for me to train for the increased distance."

"I'll bet you could do it. It would be fun, we could train together."

"It's a nice thought, but Finch is currently keeping me really busy. I'm not sure I'll have the time."

"Yeah, I heard he dumped the Mercer estate on you."

I was a bit surprised Reggie knew about that, but then news travels fast in a small law firm.

She shook her head. "Baker and Kerr should do something about him."

"They probably don't know what he's like."

A cautious expression came over her face. "They probably know more than you think about his long lunches and how little he does."

"But he brings in clients," I pointed out.

"Not as many as he used to, and there comes a point where the reputation of the firm is at stake." She paused and glanced behind her. "His three martini lunches are starting to be noticed around town," she whispered. "Sometimes he gets rather loud in public places."

I kept my face expressionless.

"Well, if you change your mind, that offer of a training partner stands."

I thanked her and she disappeared from the doorway. Before I could get focused back on my work, Phil appeared.

"How's the Mercer stuff coming along?"

I was tempted to say it would be coming along fine if people would just leave me alone long enough to work on it.

"I've just begun. It looks pretty good so far."

He nodded. "Do you have any plans for the weekend?"

Since it was only Thursday, I thought it a bit odd to be asking.

"I expect I'll be working most of the weekend on this," I said, putting my hand on the Mercer file. "How about you?"

"I'm going up to Atlantic City on Saturday to hit a couple of the casinos."

I nodded.

"You should come along with me some time. I'll show you how the games are played, and you can see how the other half lives."

"Would that be the half that's broke?"

Phil laughed. "You know my rule. Never bet more than you can afford to lose. As long as you do that, everything will be fine."

"Well, with what I'm getting paid now, that would be nothing."

"In six months, when you're an associate, we'll go up there in celebration of your promotion."

"Maybe. I'm not counting chickens before their parturition."

He frowned. "Are you really worried about not making associate?"

"Only every day when I see Finch."

"He's all bark. And, after all, you're doing half his work for him, and I'm doing the other half."

The door to the outside office slammed, and we heard Finch greeting Sherri.

"See you," Phil said, as he disappeared back to his office.

A few minutes later, before I could make much progress, I got my third interruption of the morning as Finch marched into my office.

"How is your sick friend?"

It took me a second to remember my own lie from yesterday. But before Finch could accuse me of not telling the truth, I replied, "Much better, thank you. She really appreciated my visit."

"Wonderful. Well you can make it up to me tonight by staying until I leave. That should be at around seven." He stared hard, waiting for me to make an objection.

"That will be fine. I intended to stay anyway."

"Remember, I need this by Friday of next week," he announced, and stomped out of the room.

I should have asked him if I could take a two-hour lunch like he doubtlessly would, I thought to myself, as I plunged back into the depths of the Mercer file.

A couple of hours later, I rose from the depths when my phone rang. It was Cindy.

"Just wanted to let you know that Myles and I had a real wing-ding last night, and we're not talking to each other. So I'm coming back home today rather than tomorrow."

"When are you getting home?"

"I'm guess I'll be back around six. I'm riding with a woman I met at the inn up here."

"You're not coming back with Myles?"

A loud snort came down the line. "Five hours together in the car? One of us would be dead by the side of the road before we reached Shore Side."

I sighed softly. "Well, you have a key to my apartment. If I'm not home, just come in and get Otto. I'm sure he'll be happy to see you."

"Dogs are so much better than men."

"They have their good points," I said cautiously, leaving it open as to which group I was talking about.

"Will you be home some time this evening?" Cindy asked.

"Of course. I'm just not sure when."

"Would it be all right if I came by around nine? I'd really like to talk with you about Myles and me."

"I should be home by then." For some reason Cindy considered me to be a good listener. I think it was because I never said much and stayed awake, as she rambled on about her tortured love life. Since she didn't want advice or suggestions, and I had no interest in giving either, I was the perfect confidant, although the staying awake part was frequently a challenge.

"See you later," Cindy said and hung up.

I got back to work, so intent that I ate the sandwich I had brought with me for lunch at my desk. I went to the outer office to get a cup of the coffee I had prepared that morning to have with my lunch. It might be stale, but it would keep me awake. However, I found that the pot was empty. I cursed silently to myself at the level of laziness in the office. Sherri sat blissfully typing away on her computer, apparently liberated enough to believe that making coffee was another woman's job rather than her own.

I prepared another pot.

"Mr. Finch doesn't like the smell of coffee in the office in the afternoon," Sherri said, finally deigning to notice my existence.

"He'll adjust," I wanted to snap. Instead I said, "I'm sure he'll be willing to make an exception since I have to work through lunch."

She turned back to the screen, not bothering to reply.

Sometime late in the afternoon, I heard Finch announce to the outer office that he had returned. I figured he'd close his office door and have a snooze, then do a little work until close to seven when he would go home, having kept me a captive to his draconian schedule.

Phil popped in the doorway shortly after five on his way out.

"How's it going?"

"I'm making progress," I replied.

"I see you're old school," he said, nodding toward the yellow legal pad on my desk.

"I write all my notes in longhand as I go through the materials. After that's done I put them in the computer in a more finished form."

"Very organized."

"It actually saves time in the long run."

"How far along are you?"

"By tomorrow, I should be finishing up the will, and over the weekend, I plan to start on the trust fund. By the middle of next week, I'll be poring over the balance sheets and checking the numbers."

He shook his head and smiled. "I don't envy you that job. However, the numbers have been kept pretty much up to date, so you can move along quickly."

"I hope so."

"Well, see you tomorrow," he said, giving me a quick wave.

I rubbed my hand over my eyes, which were tired from all the reading. Then I settled back in and pushed ahead. Some time later, I heard a door slam and checked the clock. It was just about seven. I went into the outer office. Everyone had apparently left. Finch's door was closed. I screwed up my courage and walked over and knocked. There was no response. I opened the door and peeked inside. Empty. Just like him to tell me to stay until he had left, then go without bothering to say goodnight.

I went back to my office and gathered my things together. I cleared off the top of my desk and carefully locked everything in a drawer. I went into the main hall to the firm's suite of offices and firmly closed and locked the main door behind me. If anything were taken, I didn't want to be the one blamed. When I walked out onto the street, it was dark. I was suddenly aware that this was the first time I had been alone in the dark since my confrontation last night with the person who followed me to the restaurant.

Would he or she try again? I walked home being exceptionally alert, looking behind me every few yards and listening carefully for the sound of feet on the sidewalk. I stayed to the side of the street with the brightest lighting and tried to keep my mind from wandering to thoughts of Luke and our enjoyable evening together. *Focus, focus*, I said to myself. Every tree with a large trunk could conceal an attacker, and someone could be lurking in every shadow.

By the time I reached the block my apartment was on, my nerves were frazzled to the point that I almost walked right past a dark clump on the sidewalk in front of the house next to mine. But then I stopped and came back. I didn't recognize it as a bag of garbage or anything that would normally be there. I walked closer. In shape it resembled a person. I switched on the flashlight of my phone.

I worked my way up from the feet to the face. It was Cindy! She was lying on her back and her face was covered with blood. Her eyes were closed, and I was certain that she was dead. However, I thought it prudent to check anyway. I put two fingers down on her neck where I thought the artery would be. I felt nothing. I pushed harder.

Her eyes popped open, and her hand grabbed my wrist.

"Who are you? Are you trying to choke me?" she asked in a rusty voice, struggling to move away from me.

"It's Madison. What happened?"

"Get me inside before he comes back," she said in a frightened tone.

"We should call the police."

"From inside!" she shouted.

I helped her to her feet and half carried her up the stairs. When we got to her apartment, Otto began to run around frantically at the sight of his mistress in distress. I got her seated on the sofa, then found a washcloth and began to wipe the blood from her face. She had a nasty cut up near the hairline on her forehead, which was bleeding badly.

"What happened?" I asked again.

"I got home later than I thought; Fran, the woman who drove me, wanted to stop in town for dinner before going on to Philadelphia. It must have been about six thirty when I got here. I went and got Otto from your place and took him out for a nice long walk, but he didn't do his business until we got to the tree in front of the Smiths next door. And you know how they are?"

The Smiths were notorious for calling the police if your dog dared to deface their property.

"I didn't have a plastic bag with me, so I brought Otto upstairs and went back out to pick up his little gift. I had just bent over, and as I straightened up, there was suddenly someone in front of me."

"What did the person look like?"

"Don't know. It was dark, and I think he was wearing a ski mask."

"But it was a man?"

"I think so. My sense is that he was taller than me by quite a bit. But I only got a glimpse because I got hit on the head right away. One minute I was on my feet, the next second I was on the ground. I lay there for a moment wondering what was going to happen next, then I must have blacked out. The next thing I knew you had your hands around my throat."

"I was checking for a pulse."

Cindy grunted.

"Did the person who attacked you take anything?"

"I didn't have anything with me except for the plastic bag." She looked at her wrist. "I've still got my watch."

"I think we have to call the police and ask them to send an ambulance."

"Do we have to?" Cindy whined. "I don't want to make a big deal out of this."

"You were *attacked;* that is a big deal. We have to report it to the police. And if you blacked out, you need to be checked out by a doctor."

Cindy started to object, but then she yawned and dozed off. I didn't think that was a good sign.

I called the police. With admirable efficiency, the police and an ambulance arrived together within fifteen minutes. Cindy's small apartment seemed rather crowded with three large men and an almost equally large woman—one of the EMTs—standing around the sofa studying her. The police asked her to tell them what happened, but she gave a diva–like wave of her hand, and said I could tell them everything they needed to know.

"Don't you want me to ride in the ambulance to the hospital with you?" I asked.

"Call Myles; he'll meet me there." She recited his number from memory, not surprising since they had been engaged longer than many people have been married.

I had some doubts about Myles' willingness to get involved, given the current state of their relationship, but while the ambulance personnel were strapping her to a stretcher, I gave him a call. He listened without speaking while I told him what had happened.

"Is Cindy going to be okay?" he asked, the concern obvious in his voice.

"I think so."

"I'll meet her ambulance at the emergency room," he said without hesitation and hung up.

I told Cindy that Myles would be there, and she smiled weakly as they wheeled her from the room. Once the door closed, I turned back to where the two police officers were staring at me intently as if they had some questions to ask.

It wasn't a pretty sight.

Chapter 5

"May we sit down?" the taller of the two officers asked politely.

Since we were in Cindy's apartment, it wasn't really my place to say, but in her absence, I decided not to quibble and nodded. I put Otto in his cage, where he flopped down looking forlorn. The two officers had introduced themselves when they first arrived, but I had been a bit flustered and couldn't remember their names. So I asked again. The tall thin one was Officer Anzelo, and the short heavy-set one was Officer Parker.

Officer Parker was the first one to speak. "Can you tell us in your own words what happened?"

I nodded, and took them through what I knew from the moment I found Cindy lying on the street. I included what Cindy had told me about the attack. They assured me that once she was in stable condition, they'd be asking her about that directly.

"Your friend said that as far as she knew nothing was taken?" Officer Anzelo asked.

"That's correct."

"And she had no idea why she was attacked or who attacked her?"

"Right."

"Do you have any idea who might want to do her harm?"

"Not at all."

"She had been out walking her dog just before it happened?" he continued.

"Yes, she came to my apartment and got Otto."

"Why was he in your apartment?"

I explained about Cindy being away and my dog minding responsibilities.

"So for the last three days, you've been the one walking the dog," the tall officer asked.

"Yes."

He glanced over at his partner. I quickly put two and two together and felt a shiver travel up my spine.

"Do you have any idea who might want to do *you* harm?" Officer Parker asked.

"Are you suggesting that Cindy's attacker might have mistaken Cindy for me? We don't look anything alike."

Parker shrugged. "You're about the same height. It was dark out and if he was looking for a woman walking a dog, it would be a natural mistake to make."

"What do you do for a living?" Anzelo asked.

"I'm a lawyer."

His eyebrow went up and again he glanced at his partner.

"Not that kind of a lawyer," I said quickly. "I do mostly wills, real estate, and tax law. I don't spend my days consorting with criminals."

"Do you have any enemies?" Parker asked.

I paused. I couldn't think of any aside from Finch, and he probably wouldn't give me enough respect to consider me an enemy.

"Not that I know of."

"Have there been any recent incidents where you've felt threatened?" Parker continued.

I was about to say no when I remembered the incident on the way to the restaurant. Reluctantly, I told them about it.

"A man was chasing you? And you didn't report it to the police?" Anzelo asked, the opprobrium clear in his voice.

"I wasn't sure in my own mind about what had happened. He could have been rushing somewhere and happened to have been behind me."

"Wearing a ski mask?" Anzelo asked, making me feel rather silly.

"I thought he was, but it was dark and I was rattled. I didn't report it because no harm was done, and I wasn't completely clear about exactly what had happened."

I wasn't about to tell them that the real reason I hadn't reported it was because I was half afraid that it had been the man I was having dinner with that night. The police would no doubt think that someone who would go out with a guy who chased her in a ski mask was certainly into kink. To be honest, I was actually starting to wonder a little about that decision myself.

"Any other incidents?" Parker asked.

I shook my head.

The two officers stood. "Tomorrow we'll check around the neighborhood and see if anyone noticed someone loitering in the area," Anzelo said. "Is there anyone who can stay with you for a few days in case you were the intended victim?"

"My only friend is Cindy," I blurted out. That sounded pathetic even to me.

The two cops shared a sad look, as if I were one step from sleeping on the street in a refrigerator box.

"Maybe you should get a room in a hotel for the night?" Parker said.

I was frightened enough to jump at the idea, but I didn't know of anyone who would take a dog. For a moment I thought about walking Otto, then leaving him in my apartment and getting a room somewhere. But he would cry if left alone at night. Suddenly the whole evening caught up with me, and I felt very tired, far too tired to go any further than across the hall to my place.

"I guess not," I said.

"We'll stay in touch," Parker assured me with a smile, and Anzelo nodded as he left.

When they were gone, I let Otto out of his cage and took him for a last walk of the night. I figured I was safe enough as long as I had him with me. As I looked up the street with its large old trees and Victorian houses that appeared elegant in the daylight but sinister in the darkness, I wondered if the attack on Cindy had really been intended for me. Cindy was a beautician, so unless she had given someone a very bad cut or dye job, I doubted that anyone was out to kill her. But then I would have said the same thing about me—until tonight.

Chapter 6

I was sitting behind my desk early the next morning when Phil popped into the doorway. He took a long look at me before speaking.

"Did you have a rough night, Madison? How long did Finch keep you here?"

"I left at seven." I was going to leave it at that, but suddenly the need to tell someone overwhelmed me and I spilled the whole story, leaving out the theory that I was the intended victim. I was shocked to find that by the end I had tears in my eyes. I hate false emotion, and I could see no reason why I, the one who had come out of all this completely uninjured, should be weepy.

"That's terrible," Phil said, coming further into my office. "How's your friend?"

"She called me this morning. They kept her overnight for observation because she had blacked out. I guess they're going to run some more tests this morning. If everything looks good, she should be able to come home after that."

"You don't expect there to be muggings on the streets of Shore Side. It's such a peaceful town. Oh, a couple of guys in a bar may get into it on occasion, and I'm sure there are domestic disputes, but basically it's a safe place. Did the thief get much?"

I shook my head. "That's what makes it so senseless. She'd just gone out to pick up after her dog and didn't even have her purse."

"Are you going to be okay to work today? Finch is watching me like a hawk since my screw up, but when he goes out to lunch, I could check out some stuff from the Mercer estate to save you some time."

"I appreciate it, Phil. But I have to do this to prove to myself that I deserve to be an associate, and even if Finch isn't here, his eyes and ears are everywhere," I said, nodding in the direction of Sherri.

"Yeah, I suppose you're right. Well, don't overdo it. Today is only Friday. You've still got next week to finish up."

"Yeah, I'll put in some time over the weekend. Have you got any big plans?"

"Getting together with some folks on Sunday to watch football; that's about it. Nothing very exciting."

"Sounds better than the Mercer estate." I said, but I wasn't sure it was true. I'm not a football fan.

He grinned and disappeared.

I was back to digging into the Mercer file again when my cell phone rang. It was Luke.

"Hi, Madison, I just got back into town a little earlier than I expected, and I wondered if it would be possible for you to have lunch with me today. I know you're probably working, and I'll understand if you can't make it." He paused and I could hear him take a deep breath. "But there's something I'd really like to talk with you about."

I had been about to put him off to tomorrow until that last sentence. I *had* to know what he was talking about. My concentration would be less than fully focused until I found out. I began to furiously rearrange the day in my mind. Finch always left for his three-martini lunch at one and usually didn't return until around three. If I left shortly after he did, I could easily be back without his noticing. Sherri would know, and she might tell him. On the other hand, she might not. Sherri was a hard one to read.

"I can do it, if you can wait for lunch until one-thirty," I replied.

"That would be fine," Luke said, with a note of relief in his voice. "I really appreciate this. I'm sure you had to rearrange your schedule."

"Nothing that I couldn't easily manage," I said airily.

"How about we meet at The Golden Porpoise?"

"The Porpoise will be fine," I said. It was only a few blocks away from my office, and I'd easily make it back before Finch.

Although my mind was only half on it, I returned to the Mercer file and slowly began to submerge myself again in the legal ins and outs. I wasn't looking forward to starting on the trust fund next week. Finch, who was manager of the fund, fancied himself to be something of an investment genius, so there were a lot of complicated transactions to trace over the more than ten years of the fund's existence. I would have to sketch all this out on a series of legal pads for tax purposes. I was thinking about the labor involved when my cell phone rang again. I saw that it was Mother's number. This seemed to be my morning to get disturbing phone messages.

I almost let it go to voice mail. My mother believes the shortest distance from one conversational point to the next is in a circle. Like a jazz player, she starts off with a theme but most of the conversation is taken up with improvisations, until she eventually returns to her point. However, I had not replied to her last few messages, and that ran a risk similar to not cooling down a nuclear reactor.

"Hello, Mother," I said.

"Well, thank goodness! I thought something terrible had happened to you when I didn't hear from you in so long."

"I've just been very busy."

"My dear, your sister Janice is *busy* raising her two daughters and taking care of her husband. Your brother Adam is *busy* as CFO of a multinational corporation. In that little law firm where you work, you are merely *occupied*."

I sighed. For as long as I could remember, my brother and sister had been the stars of the show, while I had been a supporting character actor. Being older by ten and eight years respectively, they were well along in the development of their impressive resumes before I was out of elementary school. As a child, I frequently threw tantrums over the attention they received for their more adult accomplishments as opposed to the paltry pats on the head I got for some childish achievement. All that earned me from my mother were reprimands for being envious of my siblings who had worked hard for their exalted standing, while I had yet to prove myself worthy of much of anything. As a child I had hoped that in the future I would gain an equal status. Such was not to be.

My siblings proved to be moving targets, and whatever I achieved as time went by never came close to putting me within reach of their respective pedestals. My parents, and particularly my mother, continued to think of me as an underachiever who was lacking either in talent or ambition. Which one I lacked most depended on the mood she was in at the time. It had reached the point where I believed her opinion about my lack of ambition and even congratulated myself on not being driven by a desire for wealth or fame. My siblings may have achieved more, but I was living a quiet, stress-free life of greater happiness and serenity. Most days I managed to convince myself of that, until I spoke to my mother, after which I tended to backslide into feeling lazy and inferior.

"Well, I happen to be *occupied* right now, so what did you call to talk about?"

I heard a sharp inhale and my mother continued in the overly patient tone she always used when I was being petulant. "Janice, Peter and the children are coming over for luncheon tomorrow, and I thought it would be nice if you could join us. It has been a while." She paused as if considering whether to say more, then apparently decided that to say more would be to cajole, and she never did that.

I was tempted to plead work as an excuse for begging off, but I actually consider my nieces to be pleasant little girls, and I got along pretty well with Janice, at least when we're out from under the influence of my mother. Peter is a neurosurgeon and, according to my mother, he has fixed most of the larger brains in the Philadelphia area. He's a bit of a blowhard, but he understands the power dynamics in our family and doesn't waste time trying to impress me. His goings on about what he told the Director of the Hospital or the Chief of Surgery would be directed at my parents and would be only background noise to me.

Most importantly, my mother was correct; it had been some time since I'd seen any of my family. And like them or not, they are my family.

"Peter has a meeting tomorrow morning, so we'll be eating around two."

"Okay, I'll be there," I said.

"We'll be expecting you," my mother responded, somehow managing to make it sound like a threat more than an invitation.

I went back to work with my head now divided three ways: the Mercer Estate, Luke, and my mother. As I continued to work, I slowly returned to the file in front of me, and didn't look up until I heard Finch announce to Sherri that he was going out to lunch. I glanced at the clock and saw that it was one. I dawdled at my desk for ten more minutes to make sure Finch wasn't going to reappear, then I walked into the outer office and told Sherri I was going out to lunch today.

I saw the surprise on her face and how tempted she was to ask whether I could really afford the time away from my desk. But the direct stare I gave her suppressed any thought she had of offering me advice.

It was a sunny, cool day, and I was comfortable walking along in my light jacket, enjoying the exercise after being huddled all morning behind a desk in my windowless office. I let my mind wander to what Luke had said about really needing to talk about something. Usually when a man says that, I assume he's going to break up with me, but since we'd only had one rather partial date, why bother? Luke could simply have not called me again or blown me off over the phone. Getting together to tell me he never wanted to see me again seemed a bit extreme, even sadistic. Maybe he wanted to tell me that he had a wife and five children, but really wanted to see me on the side. I'd never received that sort of proposition, but hoped I would be smart enough to turn it down.

Luke was waiting in front of the door of The Golden Porpoise looking as desirable as ever. Enough so that turning down the offer to be his piece of fluff on the side suddenly seemed more difficult. He gave me a brilliant smile and a quick peck on the cheek. A young woman walking past shot me an envious glance, not an experience I've had before. My past boyfriends have generally been middle-rung—nice enough and not ugly, but not the sort to draw admiring attention from women or men of the other persuasion on a crowded street.

We went into the restaurant and the hostess took us to a table for two by the window. I looked across at Luke, who was fiddling nervously with his napkin as if he wanted to be anywhere but here. I decided I'd been right and this was a breaking up lunch. I was about to tell him that it was okay, and he could give me whatever excuse he had prepared. I would go quietly. I wasn't one to make scenes.

"I'm afraid that I lied to you," he suddenly blurted out, staring hard as his menu as if it were written in hieroglyphics that he was struggling to interpret.

He does have a wife and kids, I thought. Imagine that! But then another thought occurred to me. What if he was about to admit that he had tried to mug me the other night, and that he had given my best friend a concussion? What is the polite way of responding to that type of admission? Do you say, "Oh, well, I'm sure you had your reasons?" Or do you casually wave his admission away and say, "Don't worry about it. No harm done." Except, of course, for the fact that Cindy was still in the hospital.

He looked up from the menu and his gorgeous blue eyes looked directly into mine. At the moment he could have admitted that he had a dozen bodies buried in his basement, and I wouldn't have batted an eye.

"I'm not really in IT," he said, and blushed with embarrassment.

I took a deep breath. This wasn't so bad. Of course, technically it was a lie, but men exaggerated their importance all the time. When a man said he was an executive, what smart woman didn't interpret "executive" to mean "lowly flunky in the corporate food chain."

I started to say something consoling, but he held up a hand to stop me.

"I'm a waiter," he said, blushing even redder. "I wasn't really out of town on business yesterday. I had to work at the restaurant last night."

That gave me pause. Plenty of men worked as waiters when they were going through school, but usually men got more prestigious jobs later on in life. Lots of mature women continued in that line of work, but men . . . not so much. Maybe this was my internalized sexism talking, but it gave me pause. Wasn't *Don't Let Your Son Grow Up To Be A Waiter,* the title of a country western song?

"I'm a very good waiter," Luke continued. "I work at Chez Molière."

"That's a very nice place," I said softly, trying to think this through.

"But you'd be embarrassed to tell people that you were going out with a waiter?" he asked, reading my mind.

I imagined the expression on my mother's face when I broke the news to her. It would be similar to the time she had bitten down hard on a peach pit. She wouldn't even be surprised that once again I had disappointed her. "Well, that's what we've always expected from you," I could imagine her saying sadly, as if I had purposely sought out a man whose job would embarrass them at the country club.

"I don't know," I mumbled. "It's just a bit of a surprise."

"I did go to college. I majored in English. I worked as a waiter in the summers and found that I liked doing it and was good at it. When I graduated, I looked around for a job, but everything I could find either I didn't want to do or it paid less, especially once I got hired at Chez."

"What do you like about being a waiter?" I asked, desperately trying to keep the conversation going while I had a chance to think.

"It's really one of the greatest service jobs there is. Just think about it, what do people do when they want to have fun and relax?"

"They go out to dinner?"

"Exactly, and it's my job to provide them with a memorable experience. And when two people who hardly know each other want to decide if they want to know each other better, what do they do?"

"Dinner," I said, nodding my head.

"Sure. For many people the most pleasant memories they have are of dinners they enjoyed at a special place with that special someone. And it's my job to make sure that those evenings go off without a hitch. I try to give them their money's worth, and at Chez Molière that involves quite a bit of money."

"I see." Luke's face had taken on an animated expression when he talked about his job. Gone were the embarrassment and the blushing. I really did understand what he was saying, but still . . .

He flashed one of his winning smiles. "So what do you think? I'd really like to keep seeing you. Do you think you could go out with a waiter?"

My mother's disapproving expression flashed before my eyes, blinding me, followed by the sarcastic comment Finch would make if he ever found out.

"I have to think about it," I stammered.

An expression of disappointment appeared on Luke's face, making me feel that I had somehow failed a test. He stood up and took out his wallet.

"When you make up your mind, I'd really like to hear from you," he said handing me a business card.

A waiter with a business card, I thought. "I will," I said. "I will let you know."

He smiled a bit sadly. He walked over to our waitress who was standing by the wall and handed her some money. She tried to refuse it, but he insisted.

She'd only given us water and menus, but I guess he felt even that any service deserved a reward, respect for a fellow professional.

I waited until Luke left. Then got up and went out, walking past our waitress.

"Sorry things didn't work out," she said. "It's none of my business, but in my opinion, he seems like a classy guy."

I paused for an instant. "Yes, he does. Doesn't he?" I said, feeling more ashamed than ever.

Chapter 7

I sat at my desk and stewed over how badly I had handled things with Luke. Sherri had been surprised when I returned so quickly from lunch, but she didn't say anything, probably because she didn't really care. I still had the sandwich I'd brought from home in my briefcase, but I didn't feel like eating anything but humble pie. How could I be so shallow? I had rejected a wonderful guy because he had a job—a job he was proud of and did well—that wasn't prestigious enough for me. I had always prided myself on being different from the rest of my family because I didn't overly value money and status. Now I had clearly proven that I was no better than the lot of them.

But the more I beat myself up for being superficial, the more I also had to admit that I wasn't brave enough to face my family and friends with a waiter in tow. My boyfriend didn't have to be a genius, a millionaire, or a neurosurgeon—but a waiter? I saw Reggie walk past my office door.

"Reggie," I called out.

She turned to come back and stand in my doorway.

"You're still engaged, right?"

She laughed. "Yeah, the last time I checked."

"What does your affianced do for a living?"

"He's a lawyer. That's how we met. We represented opposing sides in a contract dispute."

"That makes it easy. You're both professionals. No one could say that you aren't suited for each other."

"My fiancé is white."

I gave her a blank stare.

She smiled. "In case you haven't noticed I'm African American."

"Oh, yeah."

"Well, lots of folks in both our families think we are anything but suited for each other. You should have heard my grandfather. You'd think my fiancé had personally owned slaves. Jim's family hasn't been much kinder, and I know he's not told me some of the worst things they've said."

I wondered how my parents would respond if I brought home a black man. Probably it would depend on whether he had lots of money and an important job. To be fair, my parents were snobs more than racists.

"And when we go out, we sometimes run into people who stare at us like we were animals in a zoo, and sometimes a guy will make an insulting comment. Jim wants to punch him out. I have to tell him that this is what our life will be like, and he can't fight everyone."

"But how do you deal with that?" I asked.

"You learn to accept it as one of the costs of being together. If you love one another, you put up with the negatives because ultimately it's all worth it."

I thought about that.

"Do you have an inappropriate boyfriend?" she asked with a smile.

I was about to answer when I heard Finch's voice bellowing that he was back from lunch. Reggie rolled her eyes. "I'd better move along before I get you in trouble with the jerk."

She had barely left when Finch appeared in my doorway. His face was red and he was breathing as if he'd just run a race. I could see the perspiration on his forehead, even though it was a cool day. Some men are mean drunks and some men are sloppy drunks; Finch managed to be both.

"Where are you with the Mercer estate?" he shouted, as if I were a football field away and wearing earmuffs.

"Making progress," I said brightly.

"I saw you talking to your friend over there. You can't be gossiping and working. I expect you to be in here all day tomorrow. This thing needs to be finished. When I said Friday, I meant on my desk Friday morning."

"Why the rush?" I asked.

"Not that I have to give you reasons for my decisions, but the trustees are anxious to get their money. So I want you in here tomorrow."

"I have a family event that I have to go to in the afternoon. I've already scheduled it."

"Cancel it. Don't you understand, Ms. Revere, until you're an associate you've got no family? This office is your home. We are your family. I expect you here all day tomorrow, and I will be in to check."

Once Finch had disappeared back to his office, no doubt to sleep off his liquid lunch. I sat there for several moments trying to decide what to do. I'd had every intention of coming in Saturday morning, and I would still do that. But should I choose to stay in the afternoon, giving priority to work over family? Even though I wasn't particularly looking forward to the family luncheon, there was a defiant streak in me that wanted to go now more than ever.

Phil appeared in my doorway.

"I heard Finch's little rant," he whispered. "If it helps you make a decision, Finch was bragging to me earlier this morning that he's playing golf tomorrow with Judge Thorndike and a couple of his buddies. By the time they've played eighteen holes and had food and drink to celebrate the scores they've lied about, I doubt that Finch will be in any shape to come here."

"Thanks for letting me know."

Phil nodded and disappeared.

A couple hours later, as I was poring through the pages of the will, my phone rang. It was Cindy.

"How are you doing?" I asked her.

"Better. I'm back in my apartment. They released me right after lunch; apparently I didn't have a concussion. I called Myles and he brought me home."

"Is he with you now?"

"No, we had an argument, and he stormed out of here."

"What did you argue about?"

"I told him he wasn't nice enough to Otto. He said that I liked Otto more than him. And then I said, maybe I do. He's more of a man."

"I see." So it was the typical adolescent spat, which seemed to punctuate their daily lives. Although I liked Cindy because she listened to my problems and gave me psychological support in my never-ending soap opera with my mother, she and Myles brought out the childish side of each other. Alone, each was reasonably mature; together it was kindergarten time.

"When are you coming home?" Cindy asked.

I glanced at the clock. It was almost five. If I was going to spend tomorrow morning working, I certainly wasn't going to stay past six on a Friday night.

"In about an hour."

"Could you bring home some takeout, and we could eat dinner together?"

"Some Chinese?"

"That would be great."

"Okay, see you in about an hour and a half."

Right at six, I cleared my desk and got ready to leave. Fortunately, the door to Finch's office was closed as I walked across the outer office. Whether he was in there or not, awake or asleep, dead or alive: I didn't want to find out. Sherri had left at five, and the door to

Phil's office was closed. Therefore, my departure went unobserved.

I stopped at a Chinese restaurant two blocks away and placed my usual order. Since it was a Friday at six, they were very busy. I sat on a bench to wait while they prepared my food. I felt myself relax and really come down from the pressures of the day. All the conversation around me was in Chinese, so there was nothing to distract me. I closed my eyes and calmly reviewed the events.

Although I was still undecided whether I wanted a relationship with Luke, I at least felt that he was off the hook as the one who had chased me on my way to the restaurant. So he was probably not Cindy's attacker. But wait! Why did I assume that? Just because he was keeping his profession as a waiter a secret didn't mean he couldn't also be my stalker. A man with one secret might have two. Revealing his profession might just be a way to lull me into a sense of false security. No, he had to go back on the list of suspects.

But what if the police were wrong? I thought. What if chasing me on my way to the restaurant was merely a diversion, and the person who was really in danger was Cindy? But who would want to hurt her? She and Myles certainly argued like cats and dogs, but I'd never known it to get physical. I decided that over our dinner tonight I'd see if she had any ideas as to who might want to attack her.

I picked up my food and began walking home. Since it was a nice fall night, there were a number of people out on the street, so I felt relatively safe. Now, I've never been a particularly nervous person, the sort who jumps at every sound or imagines other people are plotting against her. But as I walked along, I had a distinct feeling that someone was watching me. I even turned around several times to look behind me to the point that I tripped and almost fell. Finally, I realized that the police had spooked me more than I thought with their theory that I was the intended victim of the attack on Cindy. I determined not to look around any more and to calmly walk to my destination as quickly as possible. But nonetheless, it was with a real feeling of relief that I opened the door to my apartment.

When I knocked ten minutes later, the door to Cindy's apartment opened a couple of inches and a pair of eyes peered out at me. The door flew open. Cindy grabbed my arm and pulled me into the room.

"Thank God, it's you!"

"Who did you think it would be? I'm right on time. I stopped off briefly at home to change clothes and then immediately came across the hall while the food was still hot."

"I thought it might be Myles. He keeps calling to see how I'm doing. When he last called, he threatened to come by tonight to make sure there were no lasting effects from my attack."

"That sounds very caring."

"I suppose, but he's driving me crazy. I just want to forget the whole thing ever happened, and he wants to keep reminding me of it all over again."

Cindy flopped down on the sofa and began frantically clasping and unclasping her hands in a way I'd never seen before.

"Are you sure you really are all right?"

"The doctors said so."

"It's just that you seem a bit stressed."

"You try getting hit on the head and left for dead on the street and see how you feel."

I put water on for tea and got out plates and utensils. Cindy sat quietly while I set the table.

"Sorry," she finally said. "I guess I'm more upset by this than I care to admit."

"Did the people at the hospital give you the name of a therapist you can see to deal with the after effects of the attack?"

She nodded. "Yeah. But I'll work through it myself."

Cindy prided herself on being tough and never taking abuse from people. But this was one time when she'd been attacked violently, and I wasn't certain that she was prepared to handle it.

""I'm sure you could do that," I said. "But you might heal faster with a little help."

She grunted, but didn't argue. That led me to believe that she'd already considered the idea of getting help.

We sat at the table and began to eat. I decided a change of subject might be a good idea.

"How did your vacation go? We never got a chance to talk about it."

"Vermont's a beautiful place, and the inn was great, just like a picture post card."

"Sounds wonderful."

"Yeah. You're probably wondering, if everything was so wonderful, why did I come back early."

I stayed silent. Sometimes it was better just to let Cindy take her time.

"Well, after three days, we'd had enough of each other. There just wasn't much to do except eat, talk, and walk around. And we had to do all of that together. After a while we were just driving each other nuts. I know I felt that way, and I'm pretty sure Myles did, too."

"Are you sure he's the man you want to marry?" I asked.

"That's about two days longer than I can stand being with anybody else," she said with a short laugh.

I decided not to press the issue, and we ate in silence.

"Did the police tell you any more about who might have attacked you?"

She shook her head. "They just said that it was probably some mugger who expected me to be carrying a purse instead of a bag of Otto's poop."

The police had clearly decided not to tell her their theory that she had been the accidental victim of an attack intended for me.

She looked at me and tears filled her eyes. "I think I'm going to have to move. I can't stay in a neighborhood where I don't feel safe."

"I know it's upsetting, but generally this area is very safe. I don't think you should make any decisions until you're feeling better."

"Myles wants me to move in with him, but that's not going to happen. I'd rather take my chances with a mugger."

Telling her that the attacker was probably after me might make her feel better, but there was no way to know if it was true. I was certainly not going to follow my plan of questioning her about whether she had any enemies, given the condition she was in. She didn't need to be looking with suspicion at everyone she met any more than I did.

When we were done eating, I told Cindy to rest on the sofa while I cleaned up. When I was done, she appeared to be asleep on the sofa with Otto lying across her feet. I sat in the only other chair in the room and a few minutes later my eyes began to close as well. Finally, I decided that it would be best if I went back across the hall to my own place.

"I'm going back now," I said softly. "Is there anything that you need?"

Cindy stirred. "Could you take Otto out for his walk? I'm feeling tired and a bit spooked after what happened."

"Sure." I called Otto to me and attached his leash.

To be honest, going out in the dark was the last thing I felt like doing. I hadn't been hit on the head—yet—but my nerves were stretched pretty tight. I went down the stairs letting Otto take the lead.

When we reached the sidewalk I stayed near the curb, just in case someone was hiding in the bushes or small gardens in front of the Victorians. I figured Otto would spot anyone before I would, but I kept my eyes peeled just the same. A couple of times I thought I saw humanlike shadows under the trees on the other side of the street, but when we got closer, they dissolved into figments of my imagination. Feeling rather silly, I was still happy when Otto was done, and I could make a beeline back to my front door virtually dragging the dog behind me.

I went back into Cindy's apartment. She was sound asleep on the sofa. I covered her with an afghan, figuring it wasn't worth it to wake her up to go to bed. I carefully put Otto back in his cage, and made sure the lock was on as I closed her door.

I had trouble getting to sleep, feeling guilty that Cindy may have been hurt because she lived near me. I tried to formulate a plan of action, but until the attacker struck again, there didn't seem much that I could do. With that on my mind, I finally fell asleep.

Chapter 8

The next day being Saturday, I took my time showering and having a nutritious breakfast of oatmeal, fruit, and toast. Actually, I try to eat a good breakfast almost everyday because it's the only meal I consume when I am neither under stress nor tired. Eating lunch at my desk is stressful, and by the time I get home at night, I am frequently more interested in sleep than food. So this morning was a treat. I even took my time strolling around the neighborhood a bit before setting course for work.

The door that led into Baker and Kerr's suite of offices was locked when I arrived, so I figured no one was there. But I made a point of prowling around all the offices checking to be sure. I wanted to be certain that no one who didn't belong there was lurking, waiting to pounce on me. When I felt reasonably secure, I went into my own office, unlocked my desk, and got out my materials.

I started in to work. Being relatively well rested and well fed, I made good progress as I started to pore over the figures from the Mercer trust fund. After working for a couple of hours, I felt quite confident that I would have the job completed by Thursday, so I could easily meet Finch's unreasonable Friday morning deadline.

I'd brought along a thermos of coffee from home, which to be honest, was far superior to the stuff I made for Finch every morning. He likes French roast. I think he feels it makes him seem sophisticated. But like many well-off men I've met over the years, he likes to save his pennies, so he buys whatever is on sale. I prefer Columbian for its more robust flavor, and I'm willing to pay for the best. At any rate, I had consumed a lot of it that morning, as my bladder was telling me, so I went off to the ladies' room, which is in the hall by the main entrance.

When I came out of the ladies room, I remembered that I hadn't locked the door to our suite. I'd been reluctant to do so because if someone else came in on Saturday, they'd think no one else was here if the door was locked, and I didn't want to suddenly come upon someone and frighten him or her. Now I suddenly realized that perhaps that wasn't very good security. I stopped in my tracks and turned back to lock the front door.

As I spun, I saw a dark figure duck back around the corner from where he had been watching me. I didn't wait to see who it was. Maybe it was one of my colleagues, but I wasn't about to stand around calculating the odds. I raced back to my office. I could hear footsteps pound along on the wooden floor behind me. I charged into my office and quickly locked the door. Almost immediately someone frantically twisted the knob. Since the lock was the cheap type in the door handle, I wasn't sure how well it would hold. My concern increased as a frenzied knocking on the door began, followed by a pounding, as the person seemed to throw his body against the door, which shook but held.

"I'm calling the police now," I announced in a loud voice, during one of the lulls in pounding. "I'm punching in the numbers as I speak."

This was no bluff. When the emergency operator answered, I gave my address and stated my problem in loud enough tones to be heard in the outside office. The pounding on the door stopped, but there was no way I was going to check to see if my attacker had truly left. I explained to the emergency operator that the police would find the door to the Baker and Kerr offices unlocked, and that they should come in and loudly announce themselves. Only then, would I unlock my office door and come out. She said that she would let the officers know my plan.

I sat behind my desk and waited. I wondered if he was waiting out there, gathering up his strength for another assault on my door or whether he had been frightened off by my call to the police. I also spent some time speculating on who could have followed me inside the offices. Whoever it was must have followed me from home and taken a chance by coming inside Baker and Kerr, probably betting that no one would be there on a Saturday other than myself. But that could be almost anyone.

Could it be Luke? I pictured his handsome face and winning smile. My emotions screamed "No!" but my reason said "Maybe?" I couldn't think of any reason why he would want to hurt me, but then no one else readily sprang to mind either. The only man I knew who really disliked me was Finch, and somehow I didn't see him lurking outside my apartment at night to assault me. There wouldn't be much point, because unless he intended to kill me, I would still be eligible for associate and continue as a bane of his existence.

Maybe I should dig deeper, I thought. Had I broken any hearts recently? I laughed out loud. Men usually broke up with me because I was too prickly rather than the other way around, and it had been over six months since I'd been on my last date and that was a one off.

What about something more casual—guy offering to buy me a drink in a bar, perhaps? My rather prim looks usually discouraged that, but what about when I had been out with Cindy about six months ago? She had gone to the ladies' room, and a man had sidled up to me and offered to buy me a drink. I tried to picture his face. All I could recall was short hair and large teeth, a more helpful description of a dog than a man. I'd told him that I was waiting for a friend, leaving it open whether the friend was male or female. I'd been polite but firm, and he had seemed to accept it with good grace. But I'd heard that some men held grudges when rejected. Had this man followed me home from the bar, set on getting revenge for my refusal to value his company?

I thought about it. When you started to look at the world in this way, it quickly became a very scary place. But that didn't mean it wasn't reality.

"Police!" someone shouted from the outer office.

I hopped to my feet and unlocked my office door. I rushed out looking for my saviors. There in the center of the office stood Officer Parker, the shorter of the two policemen who had questioned me the other night. I came to a halt and tried to appear calm and organized.

"Officer Parker," I said, giving him a formal nod. A quick smile passed over his lips.

"Attorney Revere," he said. "You reported a suspicious person in the office."

I explained what had happened.

"Officer Anzelo is searching the rest of the offices. How about I take a look around in here? The person you saw is probably long gone, but it's best to be sure."

He methodically went through Phil's office, Finch's office, and checked all the closets including the one behind Sherri's desk. By the time he was done, Officer Anzelo had joined us. "Nothing out there," he said.

Anzelo and Parker leaned against Sherri's desk and looked at me.

"Do you think it was the same person who chased you near the restaurant the other night?" Parker asked.

"I don't know. I did get the impression that the person was dressed in black."

"Was this person wearing a ski mask as well?" asked Anzelo.

"I'm not sure. I just saw a figure coming around the corner and I ran. I guess I've been a bit skittish lately."

"That's understandable," Parker said. "So it could have been someone who worked here?"

"But he wouldn't have chased me into my office and pounded on my door," I pointed out.

"Maybe he was concerned that he'd frightened you, and wanted to apologize," Anzelo said.

"Wouldn't he have identified himself then?"

"We're just considering all the possibilities," Parker explained. "Has anything else suspicious happened since the attack on your friend?"

I shook my head. I saw no point in mentioning that I had imagined suspicious figures all over the place while walking Otto last night. That would just lead to me being labeled as another hysterical female.

"You haven't been able to think of anyone who might want to attack you?" Parker continued.

"I really don't go out of my way to offend people," I said.

"It can happen without your knowing it. Some people are easily offended."

"No one comes to mind." I thought of Finch, but if I gave his name to the police and they questioned him, my next job definitely would be with the public defender's office—if there were a next job.

"You should have had the front door to the office locked," Anzelo said, always the critic.

I explained my theory about not wanting to frighten a colleague who came in after me. Anzelo was unimpressed. "A woman working alone in an empty office should always lock the door. That's common sense."

I hung my head, trying to act duly reprimanded. Inside I seethed. The world shouldn't have to be that way. Suddenly I felt a deep desire to find out who was harassing me and bring them to justice. I shouldn't be getting blamed for the actions of some sleaze.

Parker and Anzelo stood up. Parker gave my arm an encouraging pat. "Walk us to the door and lock up behind us."

I accompanied them to the door. As they left, Parker turned back. "Be careful after dark. Try not to go out alone. We don't have much to go on to find this guy, and he might try again."

I nodded at those encouraging words, and locked the door. I returned to my office. I was in no mood to do any further work, and anyway, I didn't have much time before I had to leave for my parents' house. The traffic into the Philadelphia area could be heavy on a Saturday, and it didn't pay to be late for a parental luncheon. It would just be another sign of my general inadequacy.

I started to put the Mercer file back into my desk, intending to come in tomorrow and put in a full day on it. But a sudden wave of fear at the thought of returning alone to the office to work made me pause. Instead I stuffed the file into my oversized briefcase, and shoved my laptop in its carrier. It was an awkward load, but worth it. I could work from my apartment as easily as from the office, and I'd feel a whole lot safer.

Chapter 9

It was good to get out on the road and away from Shore Side. Although I usually missed the quaint city whenever I crossed the canal onto the mainland of New Jersey, this time I felt that I was escaping from a bad dream. My cute Victorian neighborhood was now a source of fear for me, particularly after nightfall.

As I drove, I took Officer Parker's words to heart that some people were easily offended. I still doubted that my problems resulted from failing to appreciate a good pickup line or an unrequited romance, but there had been a few times when I'd probably offended people in the course of practicing law. Sometimes a lawyer has to tell people that they can't do things the way they wish. People occasionally take this personally, as if you were just being intentionally difficult rather than interpreting the statutes. I cast my mind back to see if I could come up with the most recent instance where this had taken place.

The last time I could think of was the Waves Restaurant case. The owner of Waves, Bill Walters, wanted to put an additional dining room on the side of his restaurant. He'd hired a contractor, Charles O'Bannon, to draw up plans and do the construction, but before Walters went ahead with the deal he came to Baker and Kerr to look over the contract. The job was assigned to me. I advised Walters that before signing anything, he should have a surveyor determine where the boundary line was between his property and the one on the side where he planned to build.

The surveyor found that the new addition would violate the required boundaries between buildings in that neighborhood, so Walters changed his mind about putting on the addition. O'Bannon, a gruff man in his sixties, had been at the meeting with the surveyor, Walters, and myself. He had been furious when Walters changed his mind about construction. I'm not certain why. Perhaps business hadn't been very brisk lately. For some reason, he directed most of his anger at me rather than in the direction of Walters or the surveyor. He said that no one paid much attention to boundaries in that neighborhood, and once the addition had been finished there wouldn't have been any complaints. He asserted that we could easily have gotten away with it.

When I said that my job was to interpret the law, not advise my client on what he could "get away with," O'Bannon had gotten even angrier. He had called me a fussy little miss who had no grasp of the realities of the business world. He balled his hands into fists and leaned forward in his chair as if he wanted to leap at me. I'd been glad that the other two men were in the room. After he stormed out, Walters had thanked me for my due diligence, and the surveyor pointed out that the neighbor could easily have sued for violation of his property rights, which might have required that the completed addition be torn down at the restaurant owner's expense. So I had left feeling that I'd done a good job. But now I wondered whether I had made a dangerous enemy, although I couldn't see how harming me would benefit him at this point in time. I thought back to the Sherlock Holmes saying that when you have eliminated the impossibilities, whatever is left, however improbable, must be the truth. I decided that, when I got back to Shore Side, I would dig more deeply into Mr. O'Bannon.

I pulled up the broad driveway of my parents' spacious suburban home outside of Philadelphia. I figured the large SUV already in the driveway must belong to Peter and Janice, which meant my mother would consider me late, even though I was fifteen minutes early. I knew I was right when she walked out on the patio from the side door and motioned with her hand as if calling a recalcitrant dog. My mother is a short and rather round woman, who clearly sees herself as tall and elegant, and therefore manages to carry herself with much more grace than one would expect. She stood in the doorway as I approached, and I resisted the impulse to curtsey. She gave me a hug, her arms releasing me quickly, as if I were a hot pot that might burn her hands.

"Peter's meeting ended early, so we are eating sooner than expected. It's good you arrived when you did," she said. I wondered if they would have sat down to eat without me if I'd only been on time rather than early. Probably so, and somehow Mother would have made it seem to be my fault.

I followed her into the kitchen and through into the dining room. Sure enough, everyone was seated around the table, which was covered in food. Janice and my father had the decency to look a shade guilty at their willingness to start without me. My two nieces, Rachel and Yvette, did them one better by jumping out of their chairs and hugging me around the waist. I stooped down and gave them both kisses.

"You shouldn't encourage children in bad table manners," my mother whispered to me. "Let's eat before the food gets colder than it is." Since the steam was rising off of the meat and potatoes, as if they were molten lava, I didn't think there was any danger of that.

As we began to eat, Mother determined the course of the conversation as she always did. The first person called upon was Peter. I could tell that he wasn't very happy about being required to report on his life as if he were a grade school student. But he dutifully talked a bit about his job, and was soon—with my mother's encouragement—expounding on a surgery he had recently performed using a new technique, and about how he planned to invent a device that would make it easier to accomplish.

"Sounds as if something like that would make a lot of money," Mother said, suddenly alert.

Peter nodded and smiled humbly, as if the advancement of medicine were his only interest in life. I glanced over at my sister. Usually she looked enthralled when Peter talked about his profession, but today she seemed surprisingly disinterested. I wondered if there was some trouble in paradise.

The conversational ball got passed to Janice. She talked about the recent accomplishments of the girls in school, but whenever Rachel or Yvette tried to add something of their own, my mother would firmly switch the conversation back to the adults. Her rule was that children could be talked about, but they weren't allowed to speak for themselves. After discussing the girls, Janice started to mention the part-time job she had begun at a local art gallery. She had majored in art history and worked as a curator at the Philadelphia Museum of Art until she met Peter at a museum event. She had quit working as soon as Rachel was born, but apparently now that the youngest, Yvette, was in school all day, she had returned to work for a gallery several hours every day.

Before she said more than two sentences about her job, Mother interrupted.

"Do you really have time for all that? In a couple of years the girls will be into all sorts of extracurricular activities. At least I hope they will or else they'll never get into a good college. You'll have to drive them around after school. That, in addition to taking care of the house and your husband, won't leave you time for a job."

"Your mother has a point," my father contributed timidly.

Usually Janice would have quickly agreed with them, but today she just looked grim. "I guess we'll have to see where things are in a couple of years," she snapped.

Mother probably would have continued to belabor the point, which was her usual modus operandi, but before she could start, Janice turned to me, "What are you up to in the legal game?"

A bit surprised at being so suddenly handed the conversational baton, I was almost at a loss for words, but I recovered as soon as I saw Mother open her mouth to change the subject. I'd had enough of being ignored as a child. I immediately launched into a brief description of the work I was doing on the Mercer estate. I could have been more entertaining if I'd talked about being stalked and almost attacked, but I didn't think that was appropriate lunch table conversation. The adults around the table seemed quite interested in what I was saying except for Mother, who was fiddling in a distracting way with her napkin.

"Well, now that we've been down into the *weeds* of the legal professional, perhaps it's time for dessert and a change of topic," Mother announced, hopping up and beginning to clear the table. Janice and I got up to assist her. As she walked past me Janice gave me a sympathetic smile. Since I only infrequently got shows of support from either of my siblings, I smiled back.

After the meal had been consumed and cleaned away, Mother, Father and Peter adjourned to the living room for more medical conversation. My father was an accountant, and I knew that sooner rather than later, a discussion would begin about how Peter might set up a business to develop his miraculous brain surgery device. Janice, the girls, and I went out on the patio. Time passed as the girls and I talked about what they were doing in school, their friends, and various other activities coming up in the future. Finally they went off to play on the swings in the yard that were still there from when my brother, sister, and I had been children.

Janice turned to me. "How do you like supporting yourself?"

I laughed. "I doubt anyone enjoys work."

"Someone who's been home with small children all day for the last eight years might."

I couldn't think of when I'd last had a serious conversation with my sister or brother, so this was entering on new terrain. I wasn't sure how to proceed.

"I can see where that might be true," I replied cautiously. "Is that why you've taken the job at the gallery?"

She smiled. Janice has always been the most physically attractive one in the family, although my brother is no slouch, and when she smiles it lights up the room, and people are immediately taken with her.

"I've taken the job out of a desperate thirst for adult conversation."

"Weren't you part of a couple of groups of young mothers that used to get together periodically?" I said, vaguely recalling previous conversations at my parents.

"Adult conversation isn't conversation with adults. It's conversation with adults about something other than their children and families. I wanted to talk about something other than childrearing and husband nurturing. At the gallery I can talk about art and the art market, something that interests me ever so much more."

I nodded. "Especially now that the girls are in school most of the day, it must get boring."

"Yes. I suppose Mother would recommend volunteer work. That's what she did as we got older. She thought it helped buttress our father's standing in the community. But I want to make some money."

"Surely Peter makes enough to support the family."

Janice looked across the yard to where the girls were competing to see who could swing highest.

"Can you keep a secret from Mother and Father?"

"Easily. I haven't confided in them since I was five."

Janice smiled. "Well, Peter and I are planning on getting a divorce."

"A divorce! Why?" I blurted out rudely. "Of course, you don't have to tell me," I quickly added. "It's just that you've always seemed so happy."

"That's just our public face. Isn't that what Mother and Dad taught us was most important? Well, it will all come out eventually. Peter has been chronically unfaithful to me."

"I always thought that he adored you."

"Perhaps he did for the first five years of our marriage," she said wistfully. "But since he's gotten more famous and begun traveling around the country giving lectures and demonstrating his surgical skills, all the adulation has turned his head. Apparently doctors have groupies as well, and now I think the only one Peter adores is himself. It's gotten to the point that I spend half my time fielding phone calls from his various amours. I don't know which I mind more, his being unfaithful or the offensiveness of having to cope with the aftermath."

"I can see why you'd want to be rid of him."

"I'm sure he feels the same about me. He can't wait to replace me with some cute young thing or two."

I looked over to where the children were playing. "It will be hard on the girls though."

Janice nodded. "That's why I'm sure that Mother and Dad will say I should ignore his wandering eye and stay with him. Not to mention the fact that it will undercut the story of happy families they love to tell all their friends."

"When will you break it to them?"

"Not today, and not in person. I want to tell Mother over the phone, so I can hang up when she begins to rant. You know what she can be like."

I nodded sadly.

"Of course you do. She's always picked on you the most. At least now she might get off your back about being the only one of us who isn't married. Also, don't tell anyone, but Jason and his wife haven't been getting along all that well either. I guess she would like to see him once in a while, and he's too busy getting ahead in business."

I thought about my brother and his picture perfect life—at least by my parents' standards—and wondered if my siblings had chosen the lives they wanted or the ones my parents wanted for them. Probably when they were back in their twenties there hadn't been much space between the two.

"So beware who you choose to marry, Madison. We come from one screwed up family."

My expression must have given me away because Janice quickly said, "Or maybe you've already made a choice."

I blushed and knew I turned a bright red.

Janice grinned. "I know we've never confided much in each other, but I've showed you mine, what about yours?"

"We've only gone out once, so it's not really serious."

"But there's something that's problematic?"

"It's his job. He's a waiter," I whispered, as if he were a level three sex offender.

Janice laughed in a most unladylike way. "Could I get you to call Mother with that news right before I tell her about my divorce? That should take a lot of the pressure off."

I found myself starting to laugh as well at the imagined expression on Mother's face after getting hit with such a double-whammy.

"Is he a good man?" Janice asked.

"I don't know him well. But I think he is."

"Well, take it from one who knows, that's what counts in the end. The money and prestige are great, but if he isn't a good man, you don't end up with much. If you can't find a good man, you're better off on your own."

I nodded, wondering if Luke was really the good man I had made him out to be. Suddenly, it was important that I find out.

Chapter 10

By the time I got back to Shore Side it was seven o'clock, and I was tired from the long drive. I had spent much of the trip brooding on how I was going to find out if O'Bannon was my stalker and how I could make certain that Luke really was a good man. I had to admit that I still harbored a niggling suspicion about him because of the proximity of his arrival at the restaurant to that of the person chasing me. I found it difficult to imagine Luke trying to injure me out on the street and then ten minutes later graciously escorting me to my seat. But my imagination when it came to men has always been rather limited, and male duplicity frequently comes as a surprise to me.

But all things considered, the Luke problem was more easily resolved than the O'Bannon matter. I had Luke's phone number. A contrite apology followed by the expression of a desire to see him again would probably get our relationship back on track and give me an opportunity to form a more accurate evaluation of his character. I was a bit stumped as to how to investigate O'Bannon. I was no Nancy Drew, and couldn't see myself staking out his home or business in my free time.

I was still working on this conundrum when I found a parking spot a few blocks from my apartment and began picking my way along the broken sidewalks toward the front door. It's rather challenging to watch your feet, while remaining on the alert for a masked attacker. No sooner had I climbed the stairs to my apartment, than the door across the hall opened, and Cindy stepped out.

"Did you have a good time with your family?" she asked.

"About what's to be expected," I replied. I'd told Cindy quite a lot about my family over time.

"I was wondering if you could walk Otto for me," she said grinning sheepishly. "I'm still a little spooked about going out there after dark."

I agreed, figuring it wasn't the right time for a bracing talk on how you should get back up on the horse that threw you.

Otto eagerly pulled me down the stairs and outside. I took a quick survey of the area, and didn't see anything sketchy. So we walked along as Otto examined and anointed a variety of trees. I actually felt quite relaxed, perhaps due to the time that had passed since the attack on Cindy. For some reason, I didn't sense that anyone was watching me. Maybe this whole stalker thing would blow over as a weird but brief episode in my life.

When Otto finally decided that it was time to go up to bed, we went upstairs. I returned the dog to Cindy and went back to my apartment. Although it had been a busy day with lots to think about, I was exhausted and happily climbed into bed a few minutes later. Very quickly I was asleep.

There was a noise in my room. I had no idea what time it was, but it felt like hours must have passed. I glanced at the clock as I tried to identify the sound. Once I sat up I realized that what I was hearing was my cell phone that was still in the pocket of the coat I'd worn to my parents. The coat was draped over the chair where I'd thrown it when I returned home because I'd been too tired last night to bother hanging it up. I jumped from my bed and fished out the phone.

"Hello," I said hoarsely.

"This is Phil; sorry to bother you, but Finch just called me."

"He wants me to come in to work now? What time is it?"

Phil paused. "Three o'clock. Apparently the office is on fire."

"On fire?" I repeated stupidly, not fully processing what was going on.

"Yeah, according to Finch the fire department is there and part of the building is in flames."

"What are we supposed to do?" I asked.

"Don't know. Finch just said that he wanted all hands on deck."

I thought comparing a burning building to a sinking ship was a bit of mixed metaphor. "Is he serious?" I asked.

"You know Finch. He sounded angry and incoherent as usual. I expect that somehow this is going to turn out to be our fault. But I think you should get up here."

I agreed to go, but took my time getting ready. I was no fireman, and if the place was in flames, there was nothing a lawyer could do except look for someone to sue.

Quite a crowd had gathered to watch the fireman direct their hoses at the blaze, which seemed to be pretty much confined to our third floor offices and wasn't nearly as dramatic as I had expected. I saw Phil standing on the edge of the crowd and went to his side.

"What's going on?" I asked.

"Not much. The only ones here are Kerr, Finch, you, and I."

"Sounds like a lot of the hands stayed below deck." I wasn't surprised Sherri stayed home in bed. She could ignore Finch with impunity.

"I heard Kerr tell Finch that there was no reason to get everyone out in the middle of the night. He and Baker didn't call any of their people."

"Just like Finch to panic and try to act like an admiral."

Suddenly I saw Finch come running toward me as if he was on fire and I had the extinguisher.

"Where have you been?" he shouted. "Don't you realize this is a disaster, and it's all your fault?"

I stared at him blankly. "What are you talking about?" I finally stammered.

"The Mercer file. I know you've been keeping it in your desk, and now it's probably been destroyed."

"She didn't have the original, did she?" a deep voice asked from behind me. I turned and saw Mr. Kerr standing there. "Company policy is that originals are always kept in our fireproof safe. We only work from copies. You did give her a copy, didn't you?" Kerr stared hard at Finch.

I could see his Adam's apple painfully move up and down as Finch tried to swallow. From his expression, I could see that he was desperately trying to come up with an excuse.

"There wasn't time to make a copy. We're under the gun to get this estate settled."

"Poor excuse, Finch," Kerr snapped.

It was an indication of how angry he was that he would reprimand a senior partner in front of us.

"The point is, what are *we* going to do now?" Finch groaned, quickly trying to spread the blame around.

"Not a problem," I said. "I brought the Mercer file home with me to work on, so it wasn't in my desk at all."

I saw a brief smile cross Mr. Kerr's lips. "I think you owe your colleague an apology and a big 'thank you', Finch."

He stared hard at Finch who eventually muttered, "I'm sorry, Ms. Revere, and thank you."

"Somehow I didn't think he was sincere. But I nodded benignly.

"Okay," Kerr said. "I've arranged for us to rent the top floor of the Ocean View Hotel. Fortunately, since the summer season is past, I was able to get it for a reasonable price. The fire is just about out, and according to the fire chief, it looks like it didn't do any structural damage to our floor. Tomorrow, as soon as the fire marshal gives us permission, I want you, Finch, to bring your SUV over here and I'll bring mine. We'll fill them with the documents from the safe and make as many trips as necessary to transport them to our new quarters."

"Sounds like dirty work," Finch said. "Shouldn't we get the associates and staff to help us?"

I knew by the word 'help' he meant we would do the tromping through the ashes and the heavy lifting, while he stood in one clean spot and supervised loudly.

"No, *we'll do it*," Kerr said, giving Finch a pointed look. "I want everyone else to be focused on getting our offices ready for Monday morning. We have appointments and work to be done. I've arranged to have office furnishings, computers, and copiers delivered before noon tomorrow. The staff and associates will be busy enough getting all that ready."

I wondered how Kerr had gotten all of this organized in a couple of hours on a Saturday night. The man truly was impressive. While Finch was all noise and bluster, Kerr quietly went about getting things done.

Kerr turned to Phil and myself. "Go home now, and get as much of a night's sleep as you can. You'll be called in the morning with information about when to report to work." He gave me a brief smile. "And keep a close eye on the Mercer file."

"I'll bring it with me tomorrow," I promised.

I made my way back home, too tired to care whether I was being stalked or not. One thing Finch had been right about, if we had lost the original and only copy of the Mercer file, it would have been a serious black mark against our firm. Normal practice would have been to keep an ongoing work copy of the original reflecting every addition and change, with the original being secured in the safe. I was sure that Kerr was seething on the inside at this breach of good practice. I wondered if Reggie was right, and Baker and Kerr were starting to think about ridding themselves of their lazy partner.

When I got home, I checked in my bag one more time to make certain that I still had the Mercer file. I knew it was there, but I was spooked. With that out of the way, I got back into my pajamas and collapsed into bed. I thought being called out to a fire might have given me new energy, but I was asleep a minute after my head hit the pillow.

Chapter 11

I got up the next morning and had another good breakfast, since I didn't have to go into work until later. Then I sat down at the kitchen table and got to work on the Mercer file. I knew the rest of the day would probably be taken up with setting up our offices. Around ten o'clock, I got a call from Sherri to come over to the fifth floor of the Ocean View Hotel because the office equipment and furniture had started to arrive. I packed up the Mercer file and my laptop and walked the five blocks from my apartment to the hotel.

It was what passed for a new hotel in Shore Side, looking as if it had been constructed in the nineteen seventies. I rode up to the fifth floor on the elevator and as the door opened I saw that an elaborate buffet had been laid out in the hall outside our suite. Phil was intently smearing cream cheese on a bagel.

"Who provided this?" I asked him.

He took a moment to swallow. "Sherri told me it was Kerr. He said we had to keep our strength up for all the moving. Figures it wouldn't be Baker, he's probably still in bed sleeping, and Finch thinks we can work without food. Not that he ever does."

Sherri came out into the hall, looking as put together as if it were a normal working day. Probably she figured that wearing a pencil skirt would prevent her being called on to move or lift anything. She stared hard at Phil and me as if we were loiterers.

"Our suite is here," she announced, pointing to an open door, and waving that we should get a move on and come inside.

"Where are the others going to have their offices?" Phil asked.

"Mr. Kerr's associates have the next suite, and beyond that is a small suite for Mr. Baker. There's another single bedroom at the end being used as a vault. Mr. Kerr is having a special lock put on the door."

I walked through into our suite. Clearly, it had originally been intended as a living room with two bedrooms off of it. In a far corner was a bathroom. The whole layout was a bit too intimate for my taste. I might have to work with these people, but I didn't want to live with them.

"I'll be located here," Sherri said, pointing to an empty spot in the center of the former living room. "She turned to Phil. You're there." She pointed to the back bedroom, which was clearly the larger of the two."

"So I'm over here," I said, drifting to the bedroom on the side. It would have made a nice nursery, but was a bit cozy for an office. One benefit, however, was that it afforded a clear view out to the Atlantic, a nice place to rest my weary eyes.

"Who set up this arrangement?" Phil asked, standing right behind me. I could see by the expression on his face that he had ocean envy. "My office looks out on the parking lot."

Sherri got that cold look in her eye that appears whenever people give her grief. "Mr. Kerr made these arrangements, so if you have an objection, take it up with him."

Phil's lips formed a firm straight line. He wasn't happy.

"I'd be happy to switch if it matters that much to you," I said.

He relaxed. "No. It's not a problem. I just thought it might have been another little punishment from Finch." Phil turned to Sherri. "Speaking of Mr. Finch, where is his office?"

"Across the hall, he has what used to be a single bedroom with his own bath," Sherri replied. "Mr. Kerr has the single next to him."

Phil and I glanced at each other, calculating the advantages of having a hall separating us from Finch. Loud noises and the men's voices came from out in that hall, and Sherri stepped out to take a look.

"Okay, the office furniture has arrived," she announced. "Mr. Kerr got them to deliver it assembled, but they won't move it from the hall into our offices, some kind of union rule because it's a Sunday. We'll have to do the moving. I looked at her tight skirt and decided that the "we" wasn't universal.

Phil and I went out into the hall. Two men had managed to fit four medium-sized wooden desks and three office chairs into the narrow hall around the buffet, which they were currently raiding.

"You're gonna have to move these into the offices before we bring up the rest," an overweight guy in a t-shirt said from the buffet table. "We can give you ten minutes. It's time for our break anyway."

"So I see," Sherri replied. I could see her weighing up the pros and cons of chasing them away from the food. She must have finally decided against it because she turned and headed back into our offices.

I studied the desk and glanced at the doorway. Fortunately, the desk was narrow enough that it could be moved into the suite without too much jockeying around. That wouldn't have been possible with the oak behemoth that I'd had in the old office.

"Two of them are mine and go in the front room," Sherri announced.

"We'll get to yours last," Phil replied curtly. "That way we won't have to maneuver around them."

Sherri pursed her lips and again decided to choose her battles.

Phil and I lifted the desk closest to the door and carried it through, being careful not to bang our fingers on the doorframe. Phil placed the desk in his office so that his back would be to the parking lot. I guessed he didn't want to be reminded of the humiliation of it all. Next we moved in my desk. I also had it placed with my back to the window. Looking out at the ocean all day would be too distracting. Also I would be looking east, which would put the sun in my eyes all morning. We continued working, moving Sherri's two desks into the front office without any difficulty, and arranging them according to her exacting specifications.

More desks arrived out in the hall. Reggie and her colleague, Stan, had shown up by now and were hauling their furniture to the proper locations further down the hall.

"This whole fire thing is really weird," Reggie whispered to me when we had a moment alone. "It must be because of something Finch has done. He must have upset someone dangerous who's out for revenge."

"You think the fire was set on purpose?"

"What do you think?"

"Old Victorians catch fire all the time."

She shook her head. "I heard the fire marshal talking to Mr. Kerr. He said they found evidence of accelerant in two locations in your suite of offices. There was no sign of anything in ours, so it must be someone out for Finch."

"I know Finch is lazy, but what do you think he could be mixed up in that would lead to arson?"

Reggie shook her head. "Maybe he's involved with the mob and hiding money for someone, maybe a person who's afraid he's going to talk too much during one of those three martini lunches."

I shrugged, not sure whether to accept Reggie's speculations. It seemed to me there would be easier ways of silencing Finch than by burning his office when he was home asleep. She walked down the hall to help Stan, the other associate who worked with Kerr.

"These go in Mr. Finch's office," Sherri said, pointing to the last desk.

Phil and I walked over to pick it up.

"That goes, too," Sherri said, pointing to a complicated looking chair.

Phil and I had gotten basic desk chairs. Finch's had an elaborate set of switches and levers like something you would find in a spacecraft.

"What's this?" Phil asked.

"An ergonomic chair," Sherri said. "Mr. Finch ordered it especially for his bad back." She turned and headed back into the suite.

"Must have cost the firm a pretty penny," I commented.

"Funny how he's got a bad back, but it's never stopped him from playing eighteen holes whenever he feels like it." Phil smiled. "I bet it would be very comfortable to sleep in after a long alcohol-fueled lunch."

I nodded, only half paying attention. My mind was still focused on Reggie's comments. What if the fire hadn't been set by someone out to get Finch, but by someone out to get me? But whether the intended victim was Finch or me, what sense did it make to set fire to the offices in the middle of the night when no one would be in there?

I walked back through our new suite, where Sherri was fussing around her desk like a proud housewife, and went into my office. I was sitting there staring out the window at the ocean, getting absolutely no billable work done, when I heard a noise behind me. I spun around in fear thinking it might be Finch, but it was Brad, the IT consultant we hire on a consulting basis, who was there to set up our computer system.

"Nice digs," Brad said, admiring my view out the window.

I nodded. "A pleasant change from that closet I was in."

"I'm afraid I wasn't able to save anything from your old computer. It was completely fried. I was able to salvage some stuff for the other folks, but your office must have been the center of the inferno. Your computer was burned to a crisp. I'm afraid you've lost everything you had stored in it."

I nodded. "Every file I was working on was also on my laptop, so that's no problem."

Old e-mails would be a loss, but fortunately I was a troglodyte and kept a hard copy of all important e-mail addresses in a notebook I carried in my briefcase. The loss of my office computer would be an inconvenience but not a disaster.

Suddenly my mind snapped back to what Brad had said.

"My office was the center of the fire?" I asked.

"Yep. Well, Finch's was pretty bad, too. I can imagine that guy has enemies, but have you ticked off anyone who likes to play with matches?"

I gave him a weak smile and shook my head.

Did that mean the arsonist was targeting me, or was it just a coincidence?

Since the only chair in the room was currently occupied by Brad who was humming to himself as his fingers danced over the keyboard, I walked through the outside office, where Sherri was still fussing over the arrangement of her desks, and out into the hall. I noticed a slight tremor in my hand as I rubbed it across my forehead.

If the fire was a coincidence, it was the latest in a long list. The almost attack on me while on my way to the restaurant; the attack on Cindy; the person chasing me across the office; the feeling of being watched at night: put enough coincidences together and you started to get a pattern, but a pattern of what? I will admit that my composure slipped for a moment and I let out a low groan.

"Get to work, Ms. Revere, the Mercer file won't complete itself," a voice behind me barked.

I turned around. Finch was walking past, carrying a box of files. He was following Kerr who was carrying twice as many. Leave it to Finch to carry a light load. His face was red and he looked distressed. The cuffs of his no doubt expensive pants were covered with gray ash from the scene of the fire. He managed to give me a final glare as he rushed to keep up with Kerr, who was twenty years his elder but twice as fit.

I wandered back to my office wondering who would want to attack me. Finch was the most likely candidate, but he was already making my life miserable well within the bounds of the law. So who else was there? I stared out at the ocean, but couldn't find any answers aside from my suspicions regarding O'Bannon and possibly—most regrettably—Luke.

I decided it was time to call Luke, for two reasons: I really did want to see him again, now that my sister had sort of convinced me that I should judge men by character rather than by wealth: and secondly, because the more I learned about him, the better idea I would have as to the likelihood of his being my stalker.

"Hi, this is Madison," I said when he answered the phone.

"Hi," he said neutrally.

I could tell by his tone of voice that this was going to be a harder slog than I had anticipated.

"I'm glad I reached you. I was afraid you might be working, since it's lunch time."

"We do brunch on Sundays, so I don't work until dinner."

"I've been thinking that maybe we could have a second date. I'd like to see you again and see how things work out."

There was a long moment of silence. "Are you sure?" he asked in a subdued voice.

"Yes."

"Okay," he said, sounding considerably less than thrilled.

"Is everything all right?"

"Yeah. It's just that you really disappointed me last time when you reacted so badly to my being a waiter. I didn't expect you to be so traditional."

"I am traditional."

He chuckled. "Oh, you look that way and sort of act that way, but I think that inside there's someone really crazy trying to get out."

I doubted that very much, but didn't think it was worth arguing about. "So what about that date?"

"I'm off tomorrow night."

"That will be fine. Let's meet at the Gray Gull Inn," I said, naming a moderately priced restaurant that I could easily walk to.

"Sounds good."

"And it's my treat."

"I can pay," he said defensively.

"I still owe you for the dog bite."

He laughed. "Okay, there is that. And I guess once your mind is made up, there's no changing it."

"I'm always open to counter suggestions," I asserted, a bit hurt that he would consider me so intransigent.

"I'm sure," he replied dryly. "Tomorrow it is then."

Once I'd hung up I realized that I hadn't told him about the fire, but then decided it was just as well. It would give us something to talk about tomorrow night, and I would be better able to judge his reaction in person.

That would make it easier to decide whether he was the arsonist.

Chapter 12

I settled down in my new office, which I already liked better than my old, and got back to work on the Mercer file. Phil stopped by an hour later and asked if I'd seen Finch recently. I told him I hadn't. Phil said he was going home. He wasn't going to waste his entire Sunday afternoon in the office when there was football to watch.

"Leaving sounds like a good idea," I responded. "I think I'll make the Friday deadline with no problem."

Phil glanced at my desk covered with papers. "Have you made a copy of the Mercer file yet?"

I shook my head. "When would I have had time to do that? I have my report on my desktop and on my laptop, but this is the only complete file," I said, waving my hands over my desk. "It would take hours to copy all of this, and that's time I'd have to take away from working on the report. I'd never make the deadline then."

"Wouldn't Sherri copy it for you?"

"Sherri wouldn't throw water on me if I was on fire; you know that."

Phil nodded sadly. "We do need more support staff."

"I figure, once I'm done with my work, I'll just put the original back in the vault because there will be no need for a copy."

"Just don't lose it between now and then or Finch will have your hide."

I nodded, trying to look fearless, but a cold chill ran up my spine at the thought of what would happen if the Mercer file went missing.

About an hour after Phil left, I realized that there were no sounds coming from other parts of the office. I walked through our suite. Sherri was gone. I went down the hall and found that all the other offices were empty and locked. Sherri had given me a key to our suite, so I decided to pack up and go home. Even though I felt safer being in a hotel, there was no sense tempting fate by remaining alone in an empty office.

I organized the Mercer file and packed it into my oversized briefcase. I slipped my laptop into its carrier, and feeling something like a pack animal, I made my way out of our office, being careful to check that I had locked the door behind me. I took the elevator downstairs, nodded to the young woman behind the hotel reception desk and went out to the street. Although I only had a walk of about five blocks, I was rather tired by the time I staggered up the stairs under the weight of all my materials. Cindy must have heard me opening my door, because she popped her head out.

"Working on a Sunday?" she asked, shocked that people did such things. I guess the beauty business functions on a more regular schedule.

I told her about the fire in our office and the need to set up a new one over the weekend.

"Probably bad wiring," Cindy said.

Ever since she'd been going out with Myles, who was an electrician, most tragedies in life were somehow related to electricity for Cindy. Just as some people blame poor diet for all health problems, Cindy considered all house disasters to be related to something called knob and tube wiring. Myles had once lectured me for a solid hour on the need to remove such a hazard from every home. I had nodded politely and immediately forgotten everything he had said, not because I believed he was wrong—Victorians were doubtlessly beautiful firetraps—but because I didn't see home ownership in my immediate or distant future. I couldn't very well harass a landlord about the need to rewire the place where I was a very temporary resident.

"You're probably right," I said to Cindy, hoping to avoid a lengthy lecture.

"Do you want to come over later? We can order pizza." She paused. "Myles and I had another fight."

I groaned inside. Cindy and Myles didn't have periodic fights; they were actually in a constant state of warfare that occasionally broke out into hostilities.

"Not tonight, Cindy," I said, feeling guilty as her face fell. "It's been a long day, and I'm going to make an early night of it."

"Another time, then," she said shortly. I could see the disappointment on her face and told myself I was a bad friend. But I knew I couldn't properly focus on the Myles and Cindy saga tonight.

I went into my apartment, changed into a pair of old sweats, and made myself some canned tomato soup and a toasted cheese sandwich. The kind of comfort food Mother would have made if she had been into comfort. By the time I was done eating, I could hardly keep my eyes focused on the magazine I had propped next to my bowl. It was clearly time to go to bed. I looked at my briefcase containing the Mercer file and recalled Phil's warning about losing it. Where in my postage stamp sized-apartment could I effectively hide it? Deciding this was a problem to be dealt with in the morning, I put the briefcase into the bed right next to me. Although not as appealing as an attractive man might have been, it was better than sharing my bed with a dog or cat, and in a few moments, I was sound asleep.

***

The next morning, while I was sitting behind my desk at work, I decided it was time to get started investigating Charles O'Bannon. I already had a date that night with Luke. Now I needed a suitable method for looking into the sketchy contractor. I looked up his construction company on the internet and discovered that it was located little more than a half mile away. But the question remained as to how I should make my approach. Nothing immediately occurred to me, so I tucked the problem into the back of my mind and returned to the Mercer file. I've found that often while I'm working on one thing, another part of my mind is busily solving an issue on the subconscious level.

An hour later, Sherri announced in a loud voice from her desk that Mr. Kerr wanted us to assemble in the hall for an all-office meeting. Phil shrugged in response to my inquiring glance as we joined those milling about in the hall. Everyone was there except for Mr. Baker, who was probably taking one of his many days off from Baker, Kerr and Fitch.

"Sorry to interrupt your work," Mr. Kerr said, "but I wanted to inform you of some important plans for the future, and this seemed to be the quickest way. The firm has today purchased a large house on Ocean Front Drive, which we plan to renovate to suit our needs. I know this may seem rather sudden, but Baker, Finch and I have been considering this purchase for some time, and the recent fire has simply expedited things. We want to complete the renovations quickly, so the firm can be moved into its new quarters shortly after the first of the year, which, as you know, is less than three months away."

Ocean Front Drive was the same street the hotel we presently occupied was on, and I wondered what my chances were of getting another office with an ocean view.

"We would like to employ a local contractor," Kerr continued, "because it would be most efficient and show our commitment to using local talent. To that end, I am requesting volunteers for a three person committee that will make a list of local contractors, seek bids, and make a short list of applicants for the senior partners to choose from by the end of the month. Anyone who is interested in serving on this committee should contact my secretary, Marion, as soon as possible."

While Kerr went on to say a few more words of inspiration about the future of the firm, I realized that sometimes your subconscious provides an answer and other times the universe just drops one in your lap. Here was the perfect way for me to legitimately approach Charles O'Bannon. As soon as Kerr had finished to obligatory applause led by Finch, I headed directly down the hall to see Marion.

"Thank God!" she said, when I declared my intention. "I told Mr. Kerr that he should simply assign three people. Getting lawyers to volunteer for anything is like getting cats to do synchronized swimming. If I volunteer myself, that means I only have to harass one other person into volunteering. That just might be doable."

"I even have a local contractor in mind who might be interested in making a bid."

"Even more wonderful." She handed me a sheet of paper and a key. "These are the specification of what the partners want done. See if your contractor is interested. If he is, take him on a tour of the house, so he can formulate a bid."

When I got back to my desk, Phil stopped by and asked if I needed any help with the Mercer file. He could come in tonight and give me a hand if I needed it.

"I have a date tonight," I said.

He smiled. "I admire your willingness to have a social life when you're under the gun."

"I'm making good progress. If I put in a productive afternoon, and spend all day tomorrow on it, I should be putting the finishing touches on the report by Thursday afternoon, and have it to Finch by Friday morning."

"How far along are you?"

"I've saved the trust fund accounts for last. I'll probably get those finished tomorrow night."

Phil nodded. "Sounds like you've got it well in hand, Madison. A good job on this should pretty much guarantee you become associate."

I shrugged. "You never know, where Finch is involved."

After Phil left, I put in a call to O'Bannon construction. The woman I talked to put me through right away to Charlie, as she called him. When O'Bannon answered the phone, I introduced myself, and told him why I was calling. Having quickly glanced over the list of specifications that Marion supplied, I summarized for him the work we wanted done. I expected him to recognize my name and cut me off at any moment, saying that all he would build for me was a sauna in hell, but he heard me out to the end. I decided that I just wasn't that memorable, even as an enemy.

"Interesting," he finally said. "That's the kind of local project I'd like a chance to bid on. Could we get together some time this afternoon to see the place?"

I had expected to have a day to think about this, but couldn't come up with a good reason to postpone. I gave him the address, and we agreed to meet there at two o'clock. When I hung up, I sat at my desk and barely avoided hyperventilating. I had just agreed to meet a man who hated me in an empty house—a man who had almost attacked me in a room with two other men present. What was I thinking? Maybe I could find someone else to come with me. I walked over to Phil's office, but it was empty.

"He's got a real estate closing, and he won't be back for the rest of the day," Sherri said in answer to my inquiry.

I considered going down the hall and asking Reggie to accompany me. She probably would, if it were at all possible, but I was reluctant to tell her that I was afraid to meet a man in a house alone just because we'd once had a confrontation. I had a feeling Reggie, the marathon runner, wouldn't need backup for that sort of situation, and although she'd agree to do it, I felt I would have diminished myself in her eyes. Women lawyers need a certain toughness to do well, perhaps even more than men.

So I was going to do it, and do it alone.

Chapter 13

I stood in front of the gracious Victorian, quaking in my low-heeled shoes and trying to remember the little I had learned in the women's self-defense course I'd taken at the local YMCA. I wasn't sure that I could gouge out an attacker's eyes or get close enough to knee him in the groin. Doing it in pantomime with dozens of supportive women looking on was one thing, but doing it alone in a vacant house was quite another. Perhaps what I needed was a weapon?

Before I could revise my position on gun control and make a quick purchase, a pickup truck pulled up in front of me with "O'Bannon Construction" on the side. A man I recognized as Charlie O'Bannon hopped out of the truck and walked around the vehicle. He had just passed the bumper when he looked up and recognized me. I knew he recognized me because he stumbled slightly and cursed softly under his breath—whether at the sight of me or because of stumbling, I couldn't tell.

It clearly took a great deal of effort for him to shorten the distance between us and put out his hand.

"So we meet again? I've forgotten your name," he said grimly.

"Madison Revere, Mr. O'Bannon," I replied, giving his hand a firm shake.

"I'm surprised that your firm would even ask me to make a bid on this project since you're representing them. I'd have figured you'd reject me out of hand."

"Actually, I thought your plans for the addition to the Wave Restaurant were very creative. My only objection centered on the boundary issue." I didn't think it necessary to add that the primary reason he was getting to make a bid was because I wanted to evaluate him as a possible stalker and arsonist.

"Let's go inside," O'Bannon suggested.

The grand central hall staircase with a mahogany bannister immediately impressed me. The floor to ceiling windows in the two spacious front rooms that must have once been dual parlors made them feel bright and airy while affording ocean views. We found a kitchen and a bath in the back of the first floor that would need serious renovations if they were to be functional. On the second floor there were five bedrooms and a bathroom. Each room was about three times the size of one of our current offices, and could easily be divided in two with room to spare.

O'Bannon walked down to the end of the hall and pulled open a door that led to a narrow stairway.

"The attic," he announced.

We climbed up the humble and poorly lit stairway and found ourselves in a rabbit warren of small rooms.

"Servants' quarters," O'Bannon said. "Probably this area hasn't been used since the early twentieth century. If we tore this all out, it would give you a lot more space for offices."

There was already twice as much space as we'd had in our burned out offices without the attic, but as I walked into one of the servant's rooms, the look out over the ocean from the third floor was truly mesmerizing. Suddenly I knew that somehow that space had to be mine.

"This is a wonderful house," O'Bannon said softly, with something like reverence in his voice.

"It certainly is," I said.

We glanced at each other, surprised to discover that we had found common ground in our love of old houses. We went down into the basement and examined the antiquated furnace and hot water heater, which elicited a laugh and a sigh from O'Bannon as he told me it would all have to be replaced.

When we returned to the main hall, he reached in his back pocket and took out a sheet of paper. They appeared to be notes from our telephone conversation.

"Here's a more accurate list of the requirements," I said taking them out of my jacket pocket.

He glanced over them. "All of this can certainly be done." He looked up at me. "But it won't be cheap if you want it done right. And to be honest, I'm not interested in doing it any other way. To do a budget job on a house like this would be a sacrilege."

"I agree," I said fervently. He stared at me in surprise. "Would you be able to complete the job by the beginning of next year?"

"Probably by the end of January, if we don't run into any major problems. The heating system will have to be replaced as I said, and central air installed. The rooms will need to be reconfigured, while still respecting their original structure. The existing bathrooms will need to be gutted, and additional ones put in. Since you want a kitchen/break area, we'll have to do a lot of work on that. The flooring needs refinishing. And there will probably need to be extensive work in the attic if you want to use it."

"We will," I said. I still had a room in the attic on my list of desires.

"And the entire building will have to be rewired."

Myles would be relieved to hear that, I thought.

"That sounds like quite a list. Are you sure it can be done in four months?"

He nodded. "Unlike most contractors, I don't lie about the timeline. I'll have several trades working at once, and put on a large crew of my own men. We'll get it done."

"That sounds good."

Charlie O'Bannon stared hard at me. "Before I go to the trouble of writing up an itemized bid, I want to know that I have a fair chance at getting the job. Are you going to go back to your employers, tell them about our last disagreement, and say there's no way in hell that they should hire me? If so, let me know now, and I'll just walk away and forget about the whole thing. No harm done."

"I don't know how many bidders there will be, but I promise yours will get the same consideration as any other."

He thought for a moment, then nodded his head. "You'll have my itemized bid by tomorrow. What's the address of your firm? I'll hand deliver it."

I told him our temporary location, and the reason why we were there.

"A fire," he said, shaking his head. "Fires are a terrible thing for old houses. A whole neighborhood can easily go up in smoke. Imagine the loss."

I nodded, starting to doubt that a man who felt that way could be my arsonist.

We left the house. I locked up and followed O'Bannon down to where his truck was parked.

He paused at the curb. "You know, I was pretty angry when you stopped me from getting that job at the Wave."

"I could tell."

He gave me a fleeting smile. "I still think we'd have gotten away with it. But I will admit that I was sailing a little close to the wind, and as a lawyer, I guess you were right to call me on it. Normally, I wouldn't have tried something like that, but times had been hard right then and I really needed the business."

"I see."

He stuck out his hand. "No hard feelings?"

I shook his hand. "None at all." *Except for the fact that I had just lost a prime suspect,* I thought.

He smiled. "Hope we get a chance to work together."

I nodded, not quite ready to commit myself until all the bids were in.

***

I was barely back behind my desk, still bemoaning the loss of a candidate for assault and arson, when my sister called.

"Well, I did it," she announced when I answered.

"Did what?"

"Told Mother about my impending divorce."

"What did she say?"

"Well, once she got over saying that she couldn't believe it—said, by the way, more in anger than surprise—and insisting that she put me on speaker phone so Dad could listen in, she pretty much told me the obvious solution was that I should ignore my husband's little indiscretions for the good of the family. I'm not sure whether she meant her family or mine."

"What did you say?"

"I told her no. I said the solution was for Peter to stop cheating on me: something which he has adamantly refused to promise."

"What did she say to that?"

Janice paused. "Mother said that I was as bad as you—always putting myself first. Sorry about that."

"Oh, well. I'm not surprised."

"But it still hurts?"

"Indeed. So where does that leave things with you and Peter?"

"He's cleared out."

"Is he living with one of his girlfriends?"

Janice gave a bitter laugh. "That would tie him down too much. He's got a bachelor pad in the downtown. I think he was actually happy to leave. Trying to keep his lies straight was probably tiring him out. I think he's pleased to be rid of the girls and me. Now he can go back to reliving his youth."

"How are the girls taking it?"

"It hasn't quite dawned on them yet what a big change this will make. Peter was away so often for business that this seems like just another trip to them. I'm sure once this all hits, it will be devastating."

I paused for a moment. "Do you think Mother would actually have taken her own advice about ignoring infidelities?"

"What do you mean?"

"If she found out that Dad was cheating on her, would she have ignored it?"

Janice laughed. "She'd have taken him for everything he owned. Propriety only goes so far for Mother. A personal insult like that would have to be avenged."

I laughed. "That's what I think, too. Do you think Dad ever did?"

"Cheat on Mother?"

"Sure. I suppose they must have loved each other once, but she really isn't very lovable in general. He's not a bad looking guy. Don't you think an attractive, kind, supportive woman might have taken a shine to him somewhere along the way?"

"I guess you never think of your parents cheating, but when you put it that way, I suppose it's possible. But if it ever happened, you can be sure he buried it deep because Mother is real good at ferreting out secrets."

"True. It's just something to think about. Did Dad say anything when you called?" I asked.

"Not a word, now that you mention it. Mother did all the talking."

"Maybe you should talk to him some time. He might be more sympathetic."

"Good idea. I'll keep that in mind."

"And I'd be happy to visit any time you want company."

"Thanks, Madison; I appreciate that."

After I hung up, I saw no point in diving back into the Mercer file. It was about time for me to leave to get ready for my date. I hadn't seen Finch since the morning and Sherri had just left for the day, so it seemed safe. I carefully packed the file in my briefcase, and put my computer in its case. I locked my desk drawer and the door to my office. I glanced in Phil's office as I left to say goodnight, but no one was there.

I walked out of the hotel and headed back home. As I strolled along, my briefcase banging against one knee and the computer against the other, I thought about the best way to keep the Mercer file secure. I could sleep with it the same way I had last night, but what if I brought Luke back to my apartment? Since it was our first real date—more of a reconnaissance mission, actually—and I hadn't fully given up the idea that he could be my stalker, I didn't plan to have him replace the Mercer file in my bed. But if things went well, I might invite him up for coffee, and I didn't want the file sitting around, just in case. When I turned up the street to head away from the ocean and toward my apartment, I realized that I would reach my car before my front door. I'd had to park a few blocks away from my house the last time I'd driven it. So why not secure everything in the trunk of my car? If my date turned out to be a bust, I could always go out and retrieve it to work on some more tonight. If I had a good time, it would be waiting for me tomorrow safely secured in the trunk.

When I slammed down the trunk and heard the reassuring click of the lock, I felt a sense of relief. At least for tonight I would be freed of that dreaded file. Now I could focus on finding out whether my new boyfriend was a crook or a really nice guy.

Chapter 14

"It's wonderful to see you again," Luke said, flashing me one of his great smiles and giving me a hug.

I figured he must have overcome some of his reservations about me since yesterday, so I gave him a brief squeeze. We walked into the restaurant and were guided to a table near the back, which was ideal because I figured we had a lot to talk about.

I'd hardly had a chance to peruse the menu when Luke said, "So what changed your mind?"

"About what?" I asked, playing dumb.

"About going out with a waiter."

"My family has always put pressure on me to marry someone rich and successful. But I've decided that character matters more than capital."

He gave me a dubious look. "That's quite a turnaround. Are you sure?"

"Of course, I'm not sure. I backslide several times a day, but I'm working on it."

"Yeah, it's not easy to go against what you've learned at home. My mom is a teacher, and she still thinks I should look for a job teaching English. Not because I'd make a lot more money, but because it's a job of more value to society. I'm not sure I agree with that, and it leads to some tense conversations. Some days I'm half convinced that she might be right."

"Yeah, parents can really screw us up trying to make us into what they want us to be."

"Usually they adjust if we're persistent enough."

"I suppose." I didn't see Mother being that malleable.

The waitress brought me my white wine and Luke his beer, and we placed our orders.

I gave Luke a careful look. "You said that you lived in West Shore Side."

"That's right."

"And you were on the way to work that night when Otto bit you?"

"Yes."

"Why were you walking up from the beach to go to work? That's a mile in the opposite direction from where you live."

Luke licked his lips and glanced around the room, suddenly seeming uncomfortable. Maybe he *had* been planning to attack me, and Otto had saved my life. I'd have to give the dog an extra ration of chow.

"Obviously, I wasn't coming from home. I'd been visiting someone."

I sat there staring at him silently. A friend of mine who practices criminal law once told me that people love to fill in silences, and you can often learn a lot by not saying anything.

"Actually, I'd been visiting a former girlfriend," he said, blushing.

"How former?"

"As of that afternoon. I'd just stopped by to see her to break things off."

I nodded, and gave him the silent treatment again.

He continued. "She wasn't happy about my being a waiter either. She wanted me to take a job in her father's business."

"And what kind of business was that?"

"He owns a real estate office."

I didn't say anything. I knew Mother would consider real estate only a small step above being a waiter.

"My girlfriend worked there as well. I thought that being in the same office with her and her father, I would start to feel trapped."

"Like maybe you had to marry her."

He nodded, looking grim. "She's kind of the possessive type. When I tried to break up with her, she kept saying that we were meant to be together."

"Is it possible," I said slowly, "that she followed you that evening after you broke up with her and saw you come up to my apartment?"

"I don't know. Maybe."

"Because the next night someone attacked the woman who lives across the hall from me when she was out walking Otto. She may have thought it was me."

"Possessive doesn't mean crazy," he said with a short laugh.

I thought about how many women had probably told themselves that before being shot by ex-boyfriends and husbands. True, women were less inclined to physical violence, but there was always the exception.

I let Luke take the conversation in a different direction, since talking about his ex was obviously distressing to him. But I filed her away in the back of my mind. We discussed his family; he seemed to have been a happy child with two brothers and a sister. His parents were obviously very different from mine because, although his mother would have preferred he become a teacher, she and his father supported their son's unusual career choice. I talked a bit about my family, leaving out the more traumatic elements. Aside from the fact that his sociopathic ex-girlfriend kept nagging at my mind, we had a good time.

When we left the restaurant, Luke offered to walk me home, which was both rather sweet and reassuring since I was still somewhat spooked about wandering around town alone after dark. As we walked along,

Luke reached out and took my hand. I couldn't remember anyone doing that since I had been in high school, and it had a certain charming innocence that I found refreshing. Although, I continued to glance around, in case his crazed ex-girlfriend was following us.

We were half a block away from my apartment when I noticed that a police car was double-parked in front of my building. I immediately pulled my hand from Luke's grasp and began to run, fearing that something had happened to Cindy. As I charged up the stairs to my apartment, I ran into Officer Parker who was standing right outside my door. He grabbed me gently but firmly by both shoulders and kept me from knocking him over.

"We're glad you're home," he said, glancing over my head and giving Luke a suspicious stare.

"What's happened?" I asked. "Is Cindy okay?"

"She's fine," Parker said. "She called us about half an hour ago because she saw someone trying to break into your apartment."

"A man or a woman?" I asked.

Parker paused as if he wanted to ask me why I thought it might be a woman, but instead he said, "Cindy couldn't tell. All she said was that it was a tall person wearing a hoodie. She only saw whoever it was from the back. When she shouted out that she was going to call the police, the person ran away. "

At that moment the door opened and Officer Anzelo stepped out.

He nodded. "Ms. Revere."

I looked at Luke, who seemed surprised that I was on such a familiar basis with the local police. I, of course, hadn't told him about the attempted attack on me when I was on the way to meet him at the restaurant the other night, since I'd half suspected him of being the perpetrator. We'd been having so much fun discussing other topics tonight, that I had also failed to mention the arson incident, and I had also not discussed with him the possibility that the attack on Cindy had been an attempt on me. In short, he was stunned, as I could tell by the way his mouth hung partially open.

Before I could do any explaining, Cindy appeared behind Anzelo.

"Are you okay?" she cried, almost knocking the officer over as she rushed to envelop me in an exuberant hug.

"I'm fine."

She glanced over at Luke and shot me an inquisitive look.

"I was out on a date."

She grinned and eyed Luke appreciatively.

"Do you have any idea why someone would try to break into your apartment?" Parker asked me.

I was tempted to mention Luke's ex-girlfriend. To come home and find a sociopath waiting in my apartment would have been disturbing. But I had no proof that she was the culprit, so I said nothing.

"Not at all. I have nothing of much value to steal."

"And no enemies that you know of," Parker said, repeating what I had told him last time.

I nodded.

Officers Anzelo and Parker glanced at each other in a knowing way that I couldn't interpret. Perhaps it was their way of saying that everyone has enemies or that I did in particular. Then they said goodnight to all of us, promising to file a report, and left.

"So where has Madison been hiding you?" Cindy said to Luke with a coy smile. I noticed she arched her back to show her figure to best advantage.

He blushed and didn't seem to know how to answer. Cindy is totally faithful to Myles, for reasons I can't begin to understand, but she likes to keep her flirting skills honed, like a retired gymnast who still walks the balance beam on weekends.

"He's the fellow that Otto bit," I told her. It was Cindy's turn to be embarrassed.

"I'm really sorry about that. I don't know what got into him."

"Not a problem. I'm fine," Luke said, flashing one of his blinding smiles.

"I can see that," said Cindy. I could swear I saw her bat her eyelashes with their false extensions.

"Let's go downstairs," I said to Luke, and pulled him away from Cindy.

We stood in front of the building and took a deep breath of fresh air.

"What's going on in your life, Madison? Why are you having so much contact with the police?" Luke asked.

I shrugged. "It just started happening a few days ago. I don't know who it is or why it's happening." I gave him a long look. "How tall is your ex-girlfriend?"

"Pretty tall. She played basketball in college. I'd say she's about five nine."

"Since Cindy is only five four, someone that height might seem tall to her."

"You think Suzy tried to break into your apartment? Why would she do that? It's me she's mad at."

"Her name is Suzy?"

He nodded.

A mature woman with the name "Suzy" was, in my opinion, bound to be unhinged.

"You don't understand much about women do you, Luke? She wouldn't come after you. She'd come after the woman who stole you away, and to her sick mind, that would be me."

Luke groaned. "This is all my fault. I never should have broken up with her. She was obviously in love with me, and now sorrow has driven her mad."

I suspected that had happened a lot earlier in Suzy's life.

"I should go back to her and tell her I'm sorry," Luke continued. "A life selling real estate can't be that bad."

"Do whatever you want," I said shortly, tired of all this self-pity. "I had a nice time tonight, up until the end. If you don't go back to Suzy, maybe we can see each other again in the future. Give it some thought."

I turned and went up the stairs to my apartment, wondering if a life of celibacy would really be so bad after all.

Chapter 15

When I got up in the morning, I suffered a moment of panic when I didn't find the Mercer file in bed beside me. Finally, I remembered that I had left it in the trunk of my car. After eating breakfast, I walked to the hotel via my car and retrieved the file. On whim, I went to work by walking along the boardwalk, enjoying the view of the ocean and the feel of the cool ocean air.

As I got to my office and settled in behind my desk, I spun around to look out at the ocean and think about Luke. The more I considered the matter, the more it seemed to me that Luke was almost as obsessed with Suzy as she was with him. Why else would he respond to my suggestion that she might have tried to break into my apartment by showing sympathy and understanding for her? What was clearly scary behavior on her part, he found easy to forgive. This was not a good relationship for him to be caught up in, but there was little I could do about it. I didn't like my chances of winning him away from his crazy girlfriend. In fact, I wasn't sure that I wanted to try. It's sad when people become emotionally attached to those who are doing them harm, but until the right moment comes, it can be impossible to rescue them.

My phone rang, and I saw that it was my mother. I almost didn't answer, but the same perverse pleasure that causes us to gawk at car accidents got me to pick up the phone.

"Hello, Madison. How are you?"

Before I could draw a breath to respond, she continued, "Have you heard about your sister's ill advised decision?"

"I assume you're talking about her decision to divorce."

"Of course, I am."

"Yes, she told me about it."

"I don't know what's wrong with that girl. She must have taken leave of her senses to break up a perfectly happy marriage like that."

"Peter is cheating on her."

"Men cheat," Mother said with finality, as if it were something she'd seen proven in Euclid.

"Does Dad?"

"Of course not," she said loudly.

"Well, I thought that if all men do . . ."

"Don't try to be funny, young lady. Can you imagine what the impact of the divorce will be on the girls? They worship their father."

"Yes. That is very sad."

"Not to mention that no one in our immediate family has every gotten a divorce."

I seemed to remember that one of my father's sisters had, but I guessed she was outside the pale. "Lots of people do," I replied.

"We aren't lots of people."

That, Dear Mother, I thought, *is exactly where you are so very wrong. We are just like lots of people.*

"I've gotten the impression recently that for some reason—God knows why—your sister now goes to you for advice. Although what you can tell her about having a successful relationship with a man, I can't imagine. At any rate, you should talk her out of this divorce nonsense before it goes too far."

"Peter has already moved out."

"I know. But men are very fragile creatures. They don't do well on their own. I'm sure if Janice asks nicely, he'll come running back to her brimming with gratitude."

I wasn't nearly as certain as Mother that this was true since, according to Janice, Peter was happily reliving his bachelor days. I certainly wanted no part of working as a go-between.

"I'll think about it," I said.

"I know what that means, Madison. It means you'll do absolutely nothing like you always have for this family."

Suddenly all the anger and stress of recent days surged through me. I held the phone away from my ear. In the distance I could just make out the sound of Mother's voice, no doubt in mid-rant on my insufficiencies as a member of the family. Not being able to make out the words felt very liberating, and it felt even better when I gently hung up the phone. She called back three times in the next minute, but I let the calls go to voice mail. Of course, there would be consequences, but I'd be better able to handle Mother in the future than I could right now.

I cast thoughts of my mother and Luke out of my mind, and spread out the Mercer file in front of me. Putting the pages I had already reviewed to one side in a pile, and what I had yet to look at on the other, I took satisfaction in seeing that the completed pile was much larger. But I was also aware that today was Tuesday and I had only until Friday to complete my work. I picked up the next section of the file and started in to work when Phil appeared in my doorway.

"How did your date go last night?"

"It had its moments, but I think he's still carrying a torch for his ex."

"Ouch! Hard to compete with that."

I nodded.

"How's the Mercer estate coming along?"

"Fine. I'm sure I'll have it ready to hand in to Finch on Friday."

"Everything looks pretty straightforward?"

"So far. There's a lot of money in this trust. I see why the beneficiaries want things settled quickly."

"There really aren't many beneficiaries left. Didn't Finch tell you?"

"No."

"When he got in touch with the trust's beneficiaries, only two of them were still alive: one of Edna's daughters and a grandson. And the daughter is in hospice care. So the way the trust reads, everything will soon go to Eric Mercer, the grandson. That's what happens when you live to almost a hundred. Many of your family predecease you."

"So is he the one that Finch says is anxious to get the whole thing settled?"

Phil nodded. "I've heard he fancies himself a savvy investor, and he wants to switch her money from the conservative instruments into something more speculative."

"Who has been managing the money in the trust fund?"

"Finch. He and Edna would get together a couple of times a year to talk about how things were doing, but Finch made the investment decisions without any outside help."

"He can't be happy at the thought of turning it over to a young guy who might well lose it all in a few years."

"Finch is hoping to convince Eric to leave a portion of the fund in his hands to manage. That way he can collect a sizeable fee. So every time young Eric comes around, Finch treats him like visiting royalty. No one can suck up to people in power like Finch."

"Or treat the powerless like peasants."

Phil nodded and disappeared.

I worked for several hours more, then took the sandwich I had prepared from my briefcase and went out to the boardwalk to eat. There was a convenient bench directly across the street from the hotel. I watched the clouds sailing along and looked out to the horizon where the ocean formed a clear sharp line of blue. A sea gull studied me from a few feet away, either hoping I was a sloppy eater or liking his chances of swooping in and grabbing my lunch. I stared hard into his beady eyes and he hopped away, aware that I was ready to defend my food.

When I came back to our suite of offices, the outer office was empty, Sherri probably having gone off somewhere for lunch and the door to Phil's office was closed. I went into my office and was startled to see a man not much older than myself, standing behind my desk leafing through my notes. He looked up as I walked in and smiled. It was a rather charming smile but with a hint of entitlement about it that I didn't like.

"Who might you be?" I asked. "And what are you doing in my office?"

He smiled some more and came around the desk toward me, completely unembarrassed. "I know this is a bit awkward, but I'm Eric Mercer. I had an appointment with Attorney Finch, but he wasn't in his office and no one was around. So I'm afraid I started wandering. Then I saw my grandmother's file on your desk, and I couldn't help taking a peek."

"Well, you should have," I snapped. "These are confidential documents, and are not meant for the eyes of anyone who happens along. We'll have it all ready for you soon enough."

The smile disappeared and I saw a steely glint come into his eyes. "I'm not exactly just anyone. As I told you already, I am Eric Mercer."

"And I don't care if you're the next in line to the English throne, this is a private office, and only a rude person simply wanders about and starts rifling through someone's things."

I'm not sure where the tide of events would have gone next. He looked ready to hit me, and I was certainly ready to slug him. But suddenly I heard Finch's voice behind me. It was a new sound. Gone was the curt, demanding tone he usually employed with Phil and myself, replaced instead by a slippery, oleaginous sound that promised groveling to new depths.

"Eric, great to see you. Very sorry I was late for our appointment. Has Ms. Revere been updating you on our progress on your grandmother's estate?"

"Actually she's been putting me in my place for looking through her notes without permission."

I could see by the malicious glint in his eyes that he was pleased to have the opportunity to get me in trouble. Obviously he was a small man when it came to character if not in body size.

"I'm sure she didn't mean to reprimand you for anything, did you, Ms. Revere?" Finch said, giving me a hard look.

"Of course not," I mumbled.

"Why don't we go in my office and have a chat?" Finch said to Eric, patting him on the back and directing him in the right direction. Finch glanced back at me. "We'll have a talk later, Ms. Revere."

Well, I probably could have handled that better, I thought to myself. But I've always had a short fuse when confronted with arrogance. I returned to work knowing that sooner or later there would be retribution coming my way. An hour later it arrived.

"What exactly did you think you were doing, Ms. Revere, insulting one of our most important clients?" Finch roared from my doorway.

"The man was poking through my files without permission. I simply asked him to stop."

"In the rudest possible way."

"I was direct, not rude."

Finch turned even redder. "I'm not sure that you can tell the difference."

That was a criticism I'd heard before from others, so I didn't respond.

"Fortunately, Eric is willing to forget the whole matter if you let him take you to dinner tonight."

"Me with him?"

"That's correct, Ms. Revere; apparently he is willing to let bygones be bygones."

"If I have dinner with him?"

Finch nodded.

I figured Eric would be expecting dinner to extend to something more. I know some people think lawyers are no better than pimps, but I was tempted to ask Finch when he had actually become one. But common sense prevailed, and I stayed silent.

"I'm sure it's an attempt on his part to get to better know the legal staff that is working on his grandmother's estate. We hope to continue to have a long working relationship with the Mercer family."

"Where are we meeting?"

"He'll pick you up at your apartment. I gave him your address. Expect him around seven."

Having said that, Finch turned and walked away. I sat there for a moment, fuming over the fact that he had been so certain I'd say yes that he had gone ahead and arranged everything. I considered my situation. Just because I went to dinner with the man, which would probably be two hours of my life flushed down the drain, it did not have to lead to anything more. With a bit of ingenuity, I could come up with a way to ward off his advances. If worse came to worst, I could always outrun him.

Since I now had a date set up by Finch, I felt no compunction about leaving right at five. I had made good headway on the file, getting well into checking the figures in the trust fund, and needed some time to prepare my mind for my encounter with the egregious Eric Mercer.

As I was walking up from the ocean toward my Victorian, I saw that a tall man was sitting on the front steps of my house. At first I thought it was Eric arriving early for our date, but as I got closer, I saw that it was Luke. He jumped to his feet as I approached and gave me a hangdog look.

"Hi, Madison."

I nodded.

"I wanted to apologize for being so weak last night. If it was Suzy who tried to break into your apartment, what she did was wrong and she should be made to apologize for it."

"It's more than wrong, Luke, it's extreme behavior. She needs help before she gets in trouble with the police."

He sighed. "I know you're right, but I still care for her in a way."

"If you care for her at all, you should talk to her about her behavior. If she won't change, you may have to talk to her parents and see if they'll intervene. Somebody has to be aware of the fact that she's going off the rails."

He nodded, but I wasn't convinced he'd heard me.

"I know last night I made it sound like I care more for her than I do for you, but that isn't true. It's just that

Suzy and I have been together for a long time, and it's hard to end something that's gone on for years."

"I understand that," I said. Of course, having never been in a long-term relationship, I understood it more in theory than in fact. "And I admire your loyalty to her. But something has to be done before she kills someone."

"I know that." Luke reached out and took my hand. "But can we still see each other?" he asked.

"Once you settle things with Suzy, we'll talk about it."

He smiled. "Thanks. I know that's all I can expect."

As he walked up the street toward the restaurant where he worked, I wondered if I'd ever see him again or whether he was going to be just another one of the men who quickly entered my life and just as quickly disappeared.

Chapter 16

The doorbell rang promptly at seven. At least he was punctual, which was more than I had expected from him. I had on my normal work attire, but with slacks rather than a skirt, in case I had to run. As I headed for the stairs I stopped by my night table, and took out the blackjack that a late friend of mine in law enforcement had procured for me. I slipped it into my jacket pocket. Most women keep items in their bedside table for arousing men; I was more interested in subduing them.

I opened the street door, and he was standing right there on the top step. For a moment I thought he was going to try to push his way inside or kiss me, and my hand quickly went to my pocket. One glance at my face and he backed up a step, managing to muster a smile. I thought even his smile verged on a leer. I walked past him, going down to the sidewalk, and heading toward the restaurant, so he had to move quickly to catch up with me.

"I appreciate your willingness to go to dinner with me," he said, gasping slightly as he tried to keep up with the pace I was setting.

"I understand from Attorney Finch that it's more in the nature of a business meeting," I replied.

He gave a short laugh. "I hoped it might be something a bit less formal than that."

I ignored the suggestion and kept walking. After travelling another block, I realized I didn't know where the restaurant was.

"Where are we going for dinner?" I snapped.

"I thought you'd never ask. We're going to The Shore Side Inn."

The same place Luke and I had gone. I'd been willing to split the bill with Luke. There was no way that I was going to do that with this guy.

We walked into the restaurant, and Eric went up to the young woman who was hostess and announced his name as if he were visiting royalty. He gave her a smile that managed to be cute and supercilious at the same time. Soon we were seated at a nice table, and I was studying the menu, looking for the most expensive selections.

He made a big production out of selecting a bottle of wine, throwing around terms as if he were a sommelier. Finally he chose something that promised to have hints of oak, leather, and bauxite, but I could have been wrong about the last one. By then I had decided to go with something from the middle of the menu in order to dampen his expectations for any excitement later in the evening.

When our salads arrived, he began to talk. It was like a spigot had been opened. He went on about the prep school he had attended, laughing at his own stories about some of the real characters he had met there who sounded like juvenile felons. He told me about his time at Harvard, which he willingly admitted had accepted him only because his father, great-grandfather, and so on back to colonial times had graduated from there. He proudly admitted having done little work and being given a diploma because of his name. From there, he had gone to work in an investment bank where his grandmother had gotten him a job. He seemed to resent the fact that they had expected him to earn his large salary, and as soon as his grandmother had died, he had quit in anticipation of his trust fund inheritance.

I have summarized what took him two hours to relate, while I asked the occasional question like an old Detroit backup singer. I insisted that we skip dessert and coffee largely because I couldn't stand his company any more, but I could tell by the gleam in his eye that he thought I was impatient to have him all to myself.

When we left the restaurant, he insisted on walking me back home. I knew exactly what his dishonorable intentions were, and was wondering whether I could politely refuse him or whether violence would be necessary. After losing two hours of my life to this bore, violence was attractive, but I knew Finch would look even less kindly on my knocking Eric Mercer unconscious than he had on my insulting him.

"You know what I really like?" he asked me suddenly, as we were strolling along the dark street.

I couldn't believe he was actually asking me a question, although I suspected that the answer was going to involve some sexual position.

"What?" I asked suspiciously.

"Muay Thai."

"Is that made with shrimp?"

He smiled with condescension. "It's a martial art. A form of Thai kick boxing. They call it the art of the eight limbs because you use all the parts of your body as weapons. I take lessons and practice several times a week. So you're absolutely safe at night when you're walking with me."

I was tempted to tell him that walking in Shore Side hardly required fists of fury, but I concluded that would be too rude. Before I could think of something more neutral to say, a figure stepped out from behind a tree about eight feet in front of us: tall, dressed in black, and wearing a ski mask. The figure said something, but it was garbled because of the mask.

"Take the mask off, Suzy," I said impatiently. "We can't understand you."

She pulled off the mask, and long red hair flowed down her back. She was an impressively sturdy looking young woman who must have spent considerable time in the gym.

"I saw you with Luke again today. Were my previous warnings not enough? Now I see you are cheating on him as well, which makes it even worse."

"Let's talk about this as rational adults . . . " I began. I decided that line wasn't going to work when she pulled an impressively long knife out from behind her back. The knife would have been even more impressive if she hadn't looked so much like a warrior princess that I had half expected it to be a broadsword.

She held the knife out in front of her as if ready to attack. I glanced over at Eric, and suddenly realized that he was gone. I looked over my shoulder and watched him as he hauled off back toward the restaurant with an impressive burst of speed. Demonstrating the art of the two limbs, I supposed.

As I turned back to Suzy, she charged forward with a rather unnerving cry like an outraged Scotsman attacking the English. Apparently, however, Suzy had never studied ballet, so her footwork was rather clumsy. Just as she had on the other night along the same stretch of uneven sidewalk, she tripped and fell to her knees. Before she could regain her feet, I stepped forward and hit her firmly on the back of her head with my blackjack. Soon she lay sprawled out full length at my feet. I took out my cell phone and called the police.

As I looked down on Suzy, I actually felt rather kindly toward her because she had relieved me of the problem of how to deal with what would have been the inevitable sexual importuning of Eric Mercer.

Chapter 17

If I hadn't needed to finish the Mercer report, I wouldn't have gone in to work the next morning. By the time the police and ambulance arrived and Suzy had been taken to the hospital for observation—and I hoped, eventual arrest—an hour had elapsed. More time was taken up with my answering the questions of Officers Parker and Anzelo. Parker, as usual, was solicitous, while Anzelo, as usual, made me feel like the whole thing was somehow my fault.

When the police asked me whether there had been any witnesses to the attack, I felt obligated to mention Eric. Not wanting to make him sound like the jerk he was, I said that he had returned to the restaurant to get help when we were accosted. Parker and Anzelo shared a dubious look when I said that, but I wasn't about to make an important client look bad. After having me repeat the entire account several times, they drove me back to my apartment and wished me goodnight. Fortunately, Cindy must have been asleep when I came up the stairs or I would have had to give yet one more rendition of the night's events.

Now I sat behind my desk, trying to concentrate, but spending most of my time looking out to sea. With the arrest of Suzy, the threats against me had now been disposed of, and I should be both relieved and happy. But I was too tired to feel either.

"May I come in?" a voice asked from the doorway. I spun around and saw Officer Parker looking as wide and solid as always. "The woman at the desk said it was okay for me to bother you."

"She's probably hoping you're here to arrest me," I said. That would make Sherri's day complete.

"Really," Officer Parker said, surprised.

"That was actually a joke—sort of."

"I didn't know you joked," he said, smiling.

"Once in a while it just comes over me. Please come in and sit down," I said, pointing unnecessarily to the only chair in the room other than the one I was sitting in.

As he settled into the chair, I studied him. He was taller than I had thought, perhaps a bit over five nine. He seemed shorter because of his broad chest and massive shoulders, which made him a presence in my small office. His face seemed nicely symmetrical, a look I've always liked in a man. I feel it makes it less likely that he'll turn out to have a two-faced personality.

"I came by to give you a report on what happened last night after we dropped you off."

I gave him an encouraging nod.

"We returned to the Shore Side Restaurant. We found your friend Eric Mercer in the bar where he had apparently been drinking for quite some time. When we told him why we were there, he immediately said, 'Madison is dead, isn't she?'"

Probably wishful thinking on Eric's part, he'd want his shameful behavior concealed, whatever the cost to me.

"When we told him you were still very much alive, he became very nervous and a bit incoherent. Some of the incoherency may have been due to the fact that he had been drinking rather heavily."

"He was probably trying to forget my death."

Parker stared at me. "You are in a rather jokey mood."

"It comes from being tired."

He nodded. "We asked him about what he had witnessed, and it corresponded with what you had told us up until the point that Mercer hurriedly left. When we told him that you had said that he rushed away to get help, he seemed a bit confused for a moment. Then he said that, of course, that was exactly what he had done."

Trust Eric to be good at shifting fields when it benefitted himself.

"We did ask him why, if he was getting you help, he never bothered to actually call the police?"

There was a question that would have made Eric sweat, I thought.

"He told us that when he reached the bar, he blacked out and had no recall of what had happened moments before. So he sat at the bar and had a few drinks, hoping to remember why he was there." Parker sat there giving me a defiant look, as if to say, "Go ahead and swallow that!"

"I suppose it's possible. The human mind does strange things when confronted with a traumatic experience."

Parker gave a small shake of the head as if amazed at what I was willing to believe.

"I have to say that neither Anzelo nor I believed him for a minute, but if you and Mercer are intent on sticking with that story, there it will remain. Mercer confirmed that the woman was intent on attacking you and that she was wielding a knife. That's enough to support the actions you took, and enough for us to book her."

"Good. That's exactly the outcome I was hoping to see."

"Suzy Ryan has admitted to attempting to attack you that night while you were on your way to the restaurant. She also admits to having attacked your friend, Cindy, believing her to be you. She also says that she did come into your suite of offices at work last Saturday and attempt to attack you."

"That helps clear things up."

Parker held a hand up to stop me from saying more. "However, she vehemently denies starting a fire in your law office or attempting to break into your apartment last night."

I thought for a moment. "I can see why she might deny the arson charge. That could be a big one. I'm not so sure why she'd balk at admitting to the attempted breaking and entering."

"Who fully understands why the criminal mind works the way it does, especially when it's someone with an obsession like Suzy's? The whole thing is crazy, so crazy that she may be able to cop a plea if she's willing to go into treatment. She's got a wealthy father to support her. In fact she's already out on bail."

"They let her have bail after she tried to gut me."

Parker smiled. "You know how it is today. If you have enough money almost everyone gets out, unless they've killed someone. But I don't think her father is going to let her get into any more trouble."

"I hope not."

"You know that guy you were out with the other night, Luke?"

I nodded.

"Well, he was there almost all of last night trying to see her and wanting to know how she was. He left the station with Suzy and her father."

"Adios," I said to myself, as in my imagination I watched Luke ride off into the sunset with a final wave of his cowboy hat. Clearly their mutual obsession was too strong for me to break.

Parker reached behind his back and took something off his utility belt and tossed it on my desk. It was a blackjack. Mine had been taken away from me last night because it was evidence.

"That isn't mine," I said.

"No," he agreed. "It's mine. I'm letting you have it because by the time you get yours back, you'll be too old to use it. That's the way evidence works."

I examined it. The new blackjack was much like my old one, but it wasn't the same.

"It's nice of you, but the old one had sentimental value. It was given to me by a friend."

"Do a lot of your friends give you weaponry as a gift?" he asked with a gentle smile.

"No, but that one did."

Parker sighed. It was deep and heartfelt. He stood up and looked across the desk at me. "Please accept my gift, Attorney Revere, in the hope that someday we can be friends, too."

I stood up, reached across the desk, and we shook hands.

"I would like that very much, Officer Parker."

***

I had settled back down to work and completely immersed myself in the various investments made over time by the Mercer trust. Most trust fund officers in my experience are pretty hands off. They make a few cautious investments and then let things follow their course unless the market gets very strange. Finch, however, had been very active in his investment strategy, so there were lots of purchases and sales to keep track of through the years. I had almost an entire legal pad of notes when Finch bounced into my office. At first I thought he was having a fit of some kind, but then I realized he was smiling widely, an expression I'd never seen on his face before.

"Good work, Ms. Revere," he announced.

"What did I do?" I asked.

"Well, I don't exactly know," he said, giving me a salacious wink, "but Eric Mercer said that he had a wonderful time last night. He told me that he is very pleased with the service he's received here at Baker, Kerr and Finch, and that he intends to leave a sizeable amount of money to be invested through us. He particularly recommended that you be made associate and assist me with his accounts."

"That's very nice, sir." I figured that now I was well on my way to getting a full time job sleeping with clients. What joy!

"Of course, I couldn't promise him that you'll get associate, but Mercer's recommendation will do a lot to incline the partners favorably in your direction. Keep up the good work." He paused in the doorway. "And don't forget, today is Wednesday."

"Yes," I said, wondering if he thought I didn't own a calendar.

"Friday morning I want the Mercer report."

I gave him a tired nod.

When Finch bounced out of the room, I sat back in my chair and smiled to myself. Eric was clearly rewarding me for my silence. Indeed, he was repaying me for the outright perversion of the truth that I had foisted off on the police. Clearly, Eric didn't mind being known as lazy, greedy, and self-promoting, but being known as a laughable coward was a step too far. That had to be kept from the public at all costs or he'd be thrown out of his Muay Thai training center with a couple of his eight limbs broken.

I relaxed and smiled to myself once again. With Suzy safely out of the way and the unexpected support of Eric, my future looked pretty bright as long as I got the Mercer file finished on time. Before I could get back to work, my cell phone rang. It was Cindy.

"Hey, how are things going? I stopped by last night but you weren't home. Have another hot date with that cute guy, Luke?"

"No, I had to go out to dinner with a client."

"Well, aren't you the social butterfly all of a sudden?"

"It wasn't quite as much fun as it sounds. I'll tell you all about it when I see you."

"That won't be tonight, which is why I'm calling. Myles wants us to have a night in tonight. I think he's feeling romantic. And the thing is, Myles gets uncomfortable with us fooling around on the sofa when Otto is watching. He says Otto stares at him and makes him feel dirty."

"Okay."

"Usually, I just put Otto out in the hall until we're through, you know. But Myles is talking about wanting to stay the night, so I wondered if I brought Otto over in his cage late this afternoon whether you could walk him when necessary and feed him dinner. And could he stay overnight with you?"

"If I can keep him in his cage when he's in my apartment. I have a lot of work to do tonight, and I can't have Otto running around like a crazy man."

"Keeping him in the cage is fine as long as you take him out for a walk."

We agreed that we'd get together in the near future, and I hung up.

It was time for lunch, so I took my sandwich out of my briefcase. At first I was going to eat at my desk, but the prospect of spending the entire day inside was not very appealing. I put on my jacket because there was quite a brisk breeze blowing. I was about to leave my office when it occurred to me that the entire Mercer file was lying exposed on my desk. Sherri often went out for lunch leaving the office unguarded. In what I knew was probably an excess of caution, I locked my office door. Then I made my way down the elevator heading for the boardwalk.

"Attorney Revere," a man called to me as I was walking across the lobby. I turned around and saw Charlie O'Bannon walking toward me.

"Hello, Mr. O'Bannon."

He rushed up to me with a broad smile on his face. "I brought my quote in to Attorney Kerr's office yesterday, and I got a call this morning that he wanted to see me. Apparently, he liked my plans so much, he's decided to choose me to do the job without soliciting any more bids."

I thought he was getting ready to hug me, so I stuck my hand out in front of me and he warmly shook it.

"There's even more," he said, his face red with excitement. "Mr. Kerr said he was going to appoint someone to be the liaison between his office and myself. I asked if that person could be you, and he said that would be fine."

That was good news on two fronts. It showed that Kerr had confidence in me, and it increased the chances that I would have significant input into the development of our new offices.

"I know you had your eye set on one of those eastward facing offices we were talking about on the third floor." O'Bannon gave me a wink. "I think an office there has a good chance of happening. Between the two of us, we should be able to secure the spot for you."

I smiled and returned his conspiratorial wink. After we talked a while more about the plans for the building renovation, I went across the street and sat along the boardwalk, eating my sandwich. I had to admit that I'd had a run of unusually good luck today, and that made me nervous. I'm better playing as an underdog. When there are overwhelming obstacles to be faced, I'm your girl, but when life is coming up roses, I begin to sneeze. The sky went from partially sunny to slate gray, which made me feel a bit better, but I was still apprehensive as I headed back inside.

I took the elevator up to our offices. Sherri was sitting at her desk as I walked in. Of course, she didn't look up or recognize my existence in any way, which was pleasantly normal. I took out my key and headed toward my office. I was about to put the key in the lock in the door handle when I noticed something odd. The area around the keyhole was heavily scratched as if someone had been trying to fit something in there to pop the lock.

I turned to Sherri. "How long were you out of the office?" I asked.

She looked at me. At first I thought she wouldn't answer, considering the question an invasion of her privacy. But she finally spoke. "I was out for about half an hour."

"Was anyone else here?"

She shrugged. "I don't know who was down the hall. But no one was in this office when I left. "Why do you want to know?"

I explained about the scratches around the lock. She came over and took a look.

"Are you sure they weren't here before?"

I considered her question. "I'm not positive, but I think I would have noticed them. I certainly didn't do it."

"I doubt anyone would try to break into your office," she said scornfully, "but these are new doors and locks. The suppliers shouldn't have sent us damaged ones like this. I'll give them a call and have it replaced as soon as possible. Does the door unlock?"

I put the key into the handle. It didn't go in as smoothly as it had before, but with a bit of twisting, I managed to unlock the door.

"Good. I'll try to get someone out here today."

"Thank you," I said. I opened the door and went inside, happy to see that everything was as I had left it.

Could someone have really tried to break into my office in broad daylight? If it had happened, the culprit must have been someone familiar with our office routine, a person who knew when no one would be in the office. Before I could give this any more thought, my cell phone rang. The screen said it was my father.

"Hi, Dad, how are you?"

"What have you been saying to your mother?" he asked angrily. Dad almost never got angry. He left that emotion to my mother.

"What do you mean?"

"Did you tell your mother that I'd cheated on her?"

"Of course not," I said quickly. Then I paused and grimly recalled the conversation.

"Well, you must have said something to her about it."

"We were talking about Janice's husband Peter. She didn't understand why Janice wanted a divorce, and I said it was because he cheated on her. Mother said that all men cheat. And I said, even Dad?"

"Oh, God," my father said almost prayerfully.

"I was trying to make the point that not all married men cheat, so Janice had a good reason for divorcing Peter. It really had nothing to do with you. What's the matter?"

"Apparently, your mother has hired a private detective to look into my relationships with women at work."

"How do you know?" I asked. I assumed that a private detective would be relatively discreet.

"One of the women who was my private secretary up until a few years ago when she left the firm was visited by a detective who asked her in no uncertain terms whether our relationship had been anything other than professional. Of course, she denied that it had been, which she could honestly do because it hadn't. But she was very upset by the inquiry and gave me a call."

"It's very disturbing that Mother would do this, but when she doesn't find anything, I'm certain that she'll calm down. There's nothing to find, right?"

"I hope not," Dad said curtly and hung up.

I didn't find that to be the rousing assertion of fidelity to his marriage that I had anticipated. Once again my attempt to make a point was having disastrous unforeseen consequences. I wondered how many children had broken up their parents' marriage by making one tiny debating point. The only good outcome was that it would take my mother's attention off of Janice and her domestic problems.

I went back to working on the file. It was turning out that the Mercer file was much more soothing than my interactions with others. It was starting to get dark outside when I heard someone come into the outside office. I didn't think any of my colleagues were around, so I picked up the blackjack Parker had left behind. Holding it behind my back in my right hand, I proceeded cautiously into the outer office. A man was examining the lock by the door into our suite.

"Can I help you?" I called out.

I must have spoken a bit louder than I had intended because he jumped, slamming into the wall.

"I thought no one was around," he said when he settled back to earth. "I'm with Jiffy Locksmiths. We got a call about a door lock that needed replacing."

"Over here," I said, pointing to the door to my office. Unfortunately, I pointed with my right hand, which still held the blackjack.

"What's that in your hand?" he asked suspiciously.

I tossed the blackjack on the top of the file cabinet as if I had no idea how it had gotten there.

"Just a bit of personal protection."

He held up his hands in front of his chest as if afraid of being attacked.

"Look, lady, I don't want any trouble. I'm just here to change a lock, nothing else."

"Fine. Go to it."

He approached me cautiously, as if I were a wild animal that could turn vicious at any minute. I backed further away from him, so he'd be more comfortable. At the rate he was moving, we'd be here all night. Finally, I went and sat behind my desk as he dismantled the door handle. When he appeared to have it disassembled, I asked, "Can you tell if anyone tried to force the lock?"

He studied it carefully. "Well, there are certainly unusual scratches around the keyhole. And I can see, now that I look inside, that the pins seem bent and there are scratches on the cylinder. I'd say somebody definitely stuck some kind of thin tool into this lock to try to force it. People don't realize that modern locks aren't all that easy to force if you don't know what you're doing. They see people use a credit card to open a door on television, but they don't realize that if you've got a door that's snug against the strike plate, you'll end up with one less credit card before you get that door open."

"What do you think was used here?"

He paused to think about it. "A very narrow bladed knife or an ice pick most likely."

I sat there thinking while he worked. I very much doubted that Suzy had escaped the supervision of her father and come here to break into my office. Even if she had escaped, her entrance into my office would have been much more dramatic and deadly. As I had concluded before, this was someone who knew our office routine. *Was someone trying to steal the Mercer file?* I wondered. But what was the point? True, the loss of the file would be embarrassing to the firm, but I was far enough along that the will could still be settled.

"All done, lady," the locksmith declared. "This is as good as new. In fact it is new."

I figured that was locksmith humor and I smiled. I reached in my wallet and handed him a twenty-dollar bill.

"What's this for?" he asked suspiciously. "I still have to charge your company for overtime."

"That's for the information you gave me. It may prove to be very helpful."

He packed up his tools and started to leave. "Be seeing you around, lady," he said, but I knew his heart wasn't in it.

Chapter 18

I walked back home in the dark. Not as nervous as when Suzy was on the loose, but not completely relaxed. There was still something suspicious going on that I suspected had to do with my work on the Mercer file. Could it be Eric, trying to steal the file for some nefarious purpose of his own or was it Finch trying to undermine me? Or was it some third person I hadn't thought of yet.

I slowly climbed up the stairs to my apartment lost in thought. When Cindy pulled her door open, I jumped.

"Sorry to startle you," she said. "I just wanted to let you know that I'm making dinner for Myles, so I haven't had a chance to walk Otto. Could you take him out in the next fifteen minutes or so? His leash is on top of the cage."

"Sure," I said, not happy about having to go out in the dark again so soon. "Did you say you're *making* dinner for Myles?"

Cindy grinned. "With my very own hands."

I was amazed. The only thing in the culinary line that I'd ever known Cindy to do with her hands was to dial the phone for takeout.

"What are you having?"

"Beef bourguignon."

I raised an eyebrow. "Sounds complicated."

Cindy shrugged. "As long as I put lots of wine in it, how bad can it be? The only foods Myles is an expert on are burgers and pizza."

"Well, good luck."

"If Otto doesn't seem happy, let me know right away."

"I wouldn't want to disturb a romantic moment."

"Don't worry; Otto comes first."

I nodded, resisting the urge to shake my head. I reminded myself—as I did many times when tempted—that it was better living alone than with a pet. I couldn't handle the responsibility. A houseplant, perhaps, but I didn't even have one of those. What all this meant for my possible future as a mother, I pushed out of my mind.

"You have no trouble keeping him in your apartment all night?" Cindy asked.

"I guess not."

"Sometimes he might snore a little, but I find it kind of soothing."

"I'm sure I will, too," I lied.

I went into my apartment and threw my briefcase and computer case on the bed. I quickly changed out of my work clothes and into jeans and a sweatshirt. I took Otto out for his walk. We didn't go far because I was anxious to get back to work. There may have been some suspicious shadows among the trees, but I felt safe with Otto along. When we got back I fed him his dinner, and put him back in his cage. He looked at me morosely, but I wasn't going to have him running around the apartment.

I popped a diet entrée in the microwave and put together a small salad. I don't really need to eat diet food to control my weight, but I find that's about as much as I can eat without feeling too full after a day at work. Cindy says I have a nervous stomach. I think all the organs in my body are nervous.

After eating and washing up, I cleared the kitchen table and spread out the trust materials from the Mercer file. Then I began the laborious process of comparing the reports provided by the brokerage houses and the mutual funds with the spreadsheets that were put in the files by the trustee manager. Everything reconciled beautifully until about two years ago when suddenly discrepancies began to appear. They were small at first, a couple of thousand dollars over a quarter, but as time went by they became larger until they reached the tens of thousands.

My hands started to shake as I went back and checked all my raw data to see if I had missed the report of some losses, but found no discrepancies. I rechecked my math, and still found no mistakes. I forged ahead until I got to the last quarter before Edna's death, which had the biggest losses of all. When I totaled up the difference between what should have been in the trust fund and what was actually there, I found that a quarter of a million dollars was missing.

I started to take deep calming breaths, but soon found myself hyperventilating. That was far too much money to be the result of an accounting error. Someone had been stealing for some time from the Mercer trust, and Haldon Finch was the manager of that trust. I thought about his three martini lunches and the rumors that swirled around the man. Plus his desk had been one of the focal points of the fire. Perhaps it had been his attempt to destroy evidence.

But as much as the finger of suspicion pointed towards him, I couldn't just waltz into the office tomorrow and accuse him of embezzlement. Even if he were guilty, he'd just fire me for incompetence and somehow find the money to cover the discrepancy. With a bit of creative bookkeeping a lawyer as skilled as Finch could make the problem disappear and me along with it. On the other hand, I couldn't ignore the numbers. Eric Mercer might well have independent accountants check over the funds reports. They would surely discover the same results that I had, and then I'd be blamed for hiding evidence of fraud. Any way you looked at it, I was running a serious risk of being fired and possibly disbarred.

My only option was to take the matter to Mr. Kerr the first thing tomorrow morning. Finch wouldn't intimidate him, and he was certainly a stickler for upholding the firm's reputation. But an ugly picture formed in my mind of a bitter argument developing between Finch and myself with Kerr acting as referee. I really didn't like my chances of winning such a confrontation. What I needed was someone else to back me up.

I picked up my cell phone and called Phil.

"Phil," I said when he answered, "I'm having a bit of trouble with the Mercer file, and I was wondering if you could come over to my place and give me some help."

"What sort of trouble?"

"I'd rather not talk about it over the phone. You really have to look at the data."

"If it's as important as you're making it sound, I'm guessing it can't wait until tomorrow at the office."

"Not really."

"Okay, I'll be there in ten minutes."

I spent the next ten minutes going over the figures yet again, hoping I'd find that I'd made a mistake. Unfortunately, everything came out showing the same two hundred fifty thousand dollar discrepancy.

There was a knock on my apartment door. I opened the door and Phil stood there. He was wearing a light jacket with jeans and a polo shirt. I didn't think I'd ever seen him looking so casual. The only sign that this wasn't a friendly visit was the briefcase he carried.

"Thanks for coming over, Phil, I really appreciate it."

He grinned. "I've offered to help you often enough, but I can't believe you've finally taken me up on it."

"I wouldn't have bothered you, but I'm getting a discrepancy between the reports from the brokerage houses and the mutual funds, and the amount that is listed on our spreadsheets as being in the accounts."

"Show me."

For the next half hour I led him through my findings. Then he told me to take a break, and he went through all the materials by himself. When he was done, he sat there slumped over the table and ran his hands through his hair.

"I get the same results that you do," he finally said. "Eric Mercer isn't going to be happy to see that a quarter of a million dollars has disappeared."

"It has to be Finch," I said.

"I never would have guessed it. But now that I think about it, he has been living a pretty high-end lifestyle for the past few years. I know the senior partners do well, but I've heard stories that he's been trying to keep up with some of his clients who are multimillionaires. Maybe he got himself seriously in debt and felt he had no choice but to steal."

I could almost feel sorry for Finch. He was the kind of guy who had to live up to a certain image he had of himself, even if it was well beyond his means to achieve it.

"What do you think we should do? I figured that maybe we could go to Kerr tomorrow and put our cards on the table. Then we could let him take care of Finch."

Phil nodded. "Kerr and Baker would probably throw Finch out of the firm—discreetly, of course—and they'd make up the missing money out of their own pockets. But things like that never stay truly secret, especially in a small city. It's bound to get out that we were the ones who threw our boss to the wolves. Being labeled snitches is not going to help our future careers."

Not being a politically savvy person, I'd never thought about that. For me it was always a matter of being honest and letting the chips fall where they may, but I could see now that there was another way of looking at the situation.

"So what should we do?"

"I think we should call Finch and tell him what we've found, and then arrange to meet together at the office tonight."

"Won't he just fire us both on the spot?"

Phil shook his head. "He'll realize that we've got the goods on him, but we're giving him a chance to make it right. The three of us will work out a plan where Finch repays the money, and nobody is the wiser. He'll be beholden to us for the rest of his career. You'll be a shoo-in to make associate, and he'll never treat us like dirt again."

"That doesn't exactly sound like Finch to me," I said.

"Do you have a better plan that doesn't get us labeled as backstabbers?"

I had to admit that I didn't.

Phil whipped out his cell phone. "Then I'll call Finch and set it up."

"Okay," I agreed, still not feeling good about the plan, which seemed a bit too slick to me.

Phil walked to the other side of the room and punched in the numbers. "Hello, Mr. Finch, this is Phil. Yes, I know it's late, but Revere and I have found some flaws in the Mercer trust fund account."

Finch must have objected to Phil's involvement because he said, "I'm only helping because Revere found a discrepancy and wanted to run it past me. We think we should all get together tonight and see what can be done about it. I know it's late, but there isn't much time to sort this out."

Finch must have asked for some specifics on the problem because Phil said, "There appears to be two hundred and fifty thousand dollars missing from the trust fund. That's right. I know it's a lot of money. No we haven't mentioned it to anyone else. We thought it best if the three of us worked it out within house."

Finch must have finally agreed. "See you in half an hour then, sir," Phil said before ending the call.

"Did he deny it?" I asked.

Phil shook his head. "He didn't say anything one way or the other. But when I gave him the exact amount that was missing, it seemed to really get his attention. He'll meet us in half an hour. I think we should get there first and be ready to show him our paperwork, so he knows that we've got him dead to rights. We need to take everything we've got with us."

He shuffled together my pages of legal notes and opened his briefcase. There was nothing in it except for a calculator and something of which I barely caught a glimpse.

"Why don't you gather together the Mercer file and bring your computer? That way he'll have no doubt we know what we're talking about."

I nodded. I put the Mercer file in my briefcase and stowed my laptop.

"We'll have to bring the dog with us as well," I said.

Phil looked surprised, like he hadn't noticed Otto before.

"Why do we have to take him?"

"He doesn't like being left alone at night. If I go out and leave him, he'll start to bark. He belongs to my friend across the hall, so she'll come running over to see what's wrong."

Phil frowned. I guessed he wasn't a dog lover. "Will he be okay riding in the car?"

"We'll have to find out, unless you want to take him across to Cindy."

"No, we'll bring him along."

I took Otto out of his cage, and attached his leash. He stared suspiciously at Phil but didn't bark. If Cindy had been alone, I would have brought the dog over to her, but I really didn't want to interrupt her romantic evening. With Phil carrying both briefcases and me handling my laptop and Otto, we quietly made our way downstairs. It was a cool night, and I was glad that I had grabbed a medium weight jacket out of the closet before we left.

Phil had been lucky in getting a parking space only half a block from my apartment As we made the walk we had to stop for a couple of moments for Otto to relieve himself. Phil seemed a bit impatient, and I have to admit that I wasn't looking forward to the meeting with Finch myself. I didn't picture it being as cordial as Phil imagined.

We drove over to the office with Otto sitting happily on my lap. I had the window open a crack, and he seemed to be enjoying all the nighttime scents. We were at the office in about five minutes.

"We should do this quietly," Phil warned. "We don't want to be seen meeting secretly."

"What about the desk clerk?" I asked.

Phil paused; apparently he hadn't considered that. He checked his watch. I knew it was almost one o'clock.

"Stay behind me," he said. "We'll check and see if anyone is on duty."

We went through the door, and he carefully peeked around the corner.

"No one is there," he whispered.

Staying close to the wall, we made our way through the small lobby and onto the elevator. The only sound was the clicking of Otto's claws on the tile floor. We took the elevator up to our office suite.

Phil opened the door to our offices and paused.

"We'd better not put on all the lights. That might be too conspicuous. Why don't you go through and put on the lights in your office. We'll set up in there."

I tied Otto's leash loosely around the back of a chair right outside my office. I turned on my desktop computer and set up the laptop on my desk. I took out the Mercer file and stacked it neatly on a far corner of my desk. All I needed were the computations I had done at home tonight. I went into the outside office where Phil was standing, apparently staring into space.

"Phil," I said, walking over and touching him on the arm. He gave a start.

"What's the matter?" he asked.

"Are you having second thoughts?"

"About what?" I thought I heard fear in his voice.

"About confronting Finch."

"No," he said. His voice was hoarse.

"I'm not sure it's the right way to go."

"I'm afraid it's the only way to go."

"Would you give me my legal sheets of figures from your briefcase?"

He nodded and opened the case. There was a flash of light off something. I took the papers and returned to my office. I sat at my desk and found the last section of my report that was on the laptop. If our meeting with Finch fell through, I'd be completing my report tomorrow and possibly ending my employment at Baker, Kerr, and Finch.

Phil appeared in my doorway as he had so many times before. I could see by my office light that he looked tired, haggard even. This was taking as much of a toll on him as it was on me.

"Would you show me where your report left off?" he asked.

I nodded and he walked over to stand behind me. I scrolled down to the last sentence I had written. As I read it over, I saw a flash of light off whatever was in Phil's right hand, and suddenly it clicked with me what I had seen in Phil's briefcase: an ice pick.

I slammed my chair back hard into Phil, shoving him into the window. Before he could recover I darted out from behind my desk heading for the outer office. I knew that with luck and a little room I could outrun him. But then I heard Otto bark in that same menacing way he'd used when he'd attacked Luke. I spun around in time to see Phil come charging out of my office with the ice pick raised high in his hand. Before he took more than a couple of steps, Otto pulled his leash loose from the chair and attacked. Fixing his teeth into Phil's left leg, he spun him around. Surprised by the dog's charge, Phil was doing a jerky dance with Otto, and I could see that he was trying to get an angle to plunge the ice pick into the dog's neck.

I went around the two of them to the file cabinet where I had absentmindedly left the blackjack earlier that evening. I stood behind Phil, just as he raised his arm to plunge the ice pick into Otto. I swung the blackjack with all of my might, bringing it down hard on the top of Phil's shoulder. I heard something crack as the blow struck. His arm went limp and the ice pick fell to the floor. Phil tried to turn towards me, but I gave him a slightly gentler tap on the back of the head and he collapsed on the floor.

I pulled Otto away from Phil's leg, which he was still gnawing on with enthusiasm, and tied him up again on the other side of the office. Then for the second time in as many nights I called the police.

Chapter 19

I went to work the next day as if nothing had happened. I think I had a superstitious feeling that if I pretended that nothing had happened, reality would adjust itself that way. And actually it *was* as if nothing had happened. I sat at my desk working on an honest report about the Mercer trust, getting ready to turn it in Friday morning. Actually with all the effort I'd put in last night, it was going to be done early, probably by the afternoon. But I had learned that as a lawyer you never complete anything early or else no one believes that you worked hard enough.

I wasn't certain to whom I was going to give my report. Phil, of course, had not come in to work. Finch arrived at his usual time, but I saw Mr. Kerr go into his office and the two men disappeared down the hall into Kerr's office. Finch didn't reappear for the rest of the day.

Sherri seemed to be a person lost. She came into my office at nine wanting to know where Phil was, and I told her I didn't know. She came back at eleven to ask if I knew where Finch was. Asking me where her beloved boss was must have cost her a lot, but again I couldn't help her. She sat at her desk for the rest of the day listlessly sorting through files. I almost felt sorry for her.

Last night Parker and Anzelo had shown up and taken my statement. I had given them a very detailed account of the events leading up to the attack on me because I wanted someone other than myself to know about the financial shenanigans that had led to it. Phil had disappeared under guard in an ambulance, and after my statement, they had given Otto and me a ride back home. In the morning, I walked Otto and gave him some food, but I didn't return him to Cindy. She had a key and could pick him up herself. From what I could hear through the door, the lovebirds were back to fighting again.

I had managed to piece together some of what had happened by thinking about what I knew. It was now obvious to me that it was Phil who had been stealing the money from the trust. Finch had largely delegated his managerial responsibilities to Phil for the past two years, and he was probably unaware of what Phil had been doing. So when I had called Phil to help me, I'd been notifying the fox that I'd spotted the carnage in the henhouse. Not my smartest move. In my own defense, I'd let my dislike of Finch color my perceptions. Also, I now realized that Phil had only pretended to call Finch last night and set up a meeting. His plan had all along been to get me alone in the office, kill me, and destroy the Mercer file along with my laptop and office computer. That way all proof of his crime would be eradicated.

Because of Phil's use of an ice pick as an attempted murder weapon, I was also pretty certain that he had tried to break into my office in order to steal and destroy the Mercer file. I could only imagine what a shock it had been to him when Finch had assigned that project to me. Phil might have been able to cover up his theft if he had been given the file, but once it was assigned to me his goose had gone into the oven. As a sign of how desperate he was, he had even torched our offices in the hopes of destroying the evidence. I'm sure he had felt that the universe was against him when I told Finch that it was safely at my apartment. That had led to his attempt to break into my apartment, which was thwarted by the ever-alert Cindy.

Suzy had actually been telling the truth when she denied being an arsonist or a break-in artist. She had been nothing more than your garden-variety sociopath. Again, I wished Luke luck in reforming her.

So by the end of the day, as I packed my things—for once leaving the Mercer file locked in my desk—and headed out, I thought that aside from a few uncrossed t's and undotted i's, I pretty much knew what had happened.

"Ms. Revere," a voice called, as I was about to step on the elevator. I turned and saw Mr. Kerr heading down the hallway toward me at a rapid clip. "Could I speak with you for a few minutes in my office?"

When the big boss says that, it's not really a request in the truest sense of the word. I followed him into his office and sat docilely in front of his desk. He settled into his chair but didn't say anything for a moment. It took me a second before I realized that he was at a loss for words. Perhaps, this whole incident had been so embarrassing that he didn't know how to begin. I would have helped him, but there was nothing I could say to help to soften the blow to the firm's reputation. It wasn't exactly his fault, but when you're the head man, everything is your fault.

He cleared his throat. "I guess you must be very near the completion of your report on the Mercer will and trust fund."

"I'll be handing it in tomorrow morning as requested by Mr. Finch."

"Good. I understand that your report will show that there were certain monies withdrawn from the trust fund without authorization."

"How do you know that?" I asked.

"Phil admitted as much to me at the hospital last night."

"I finally figured out that he must have been the culprit, although I was a bit slow on the uptake."

"You were ahead of the rest of us," Kerr said dryly.

"Why did Phil do it?"

"He told me had had huge gambling debts at a couple of casinos."

"He told me he never bet more than he could afford to lose."

Mr. Kerr shrugged. "I'm sure every addict tells themselves that."

"What happens next?" I asked

"None of this is to become public knowledge. Mr. Finch has recognized his failure to supervise the trust properly, and he has agreed to restore the missing monies from his own account. Neither the Mercers nor anyone else need be any the wiser."

"How are you going to explain Phil's attack on me last night?"

"He is being charged with assault with a deadly weapon."

"Not attempted murder?"

A pained expression came over Kerr's face. "Baker and I had a chat with the district attorney, and he agreed that it would be better to bring the lesser charge since Phil is willing to plead guilty to it. No one wants to waste public money on a prolonged trial."

I barely controlled my anger. "I'm sure it would be better for the firm as well. There will be much less publicity. Just don't forget that in reality he tried to drive an ice pick into my brain."

Kerr shifted uneasily in his chair. "I am aware of that," he said softly, "and I deeply regret the ordeal you had to go through."

"But, again, what reason are you giving for the attack?"

Kerr gave me a meaningful look. "Phil had a breakdown of some sort that led him to attack you. He'd been working very hard and became unbalanced."

I thought about how fast and loose we were playing with the truth. The whole thing made me uncomfortable. Kerr must have read my mind.

"Baker and I know that you are a loyal member of the firm and have done very good work in your brief time here. As a sign of our commitment to you, we are willing to advance you to associate several months early." He smiled. "After all, we do need an associate to replace Phil. Your salary will be increased to reflect your new position."

"How does Mr. Finch feel about this?" I couldn't imagine him being happy with my untimely advancement.

Kerr cleared his throat once again. "Mr. Finch has decided to leave the firm in order to pursue other avenues."

I'm sure the surprise was evident on my face. "Whom will I be working for, then?"

"You will be working in my office and reporting directly to me."

"I see." I was a bit stunned, but I knew it would be better than working with Finch.

"That will also allow us to coordinate more easily on the renovations for the new offices," he said with a smile. "According to Mr. O'Bannon you have a special interest in the third floor. I'm sure all of that can easily be worked out."

I warned myself not to share anything with O'Bannon that I didn't want to become public knowledge.

So there it was, I had been thoroughly bribed with a new title, a salary increase, a better boss, and the promise of the office of my dreams. I wasn't completely happy about the truth being concealed, but then there was little to be gained in telling Eric that Phil had tried to steal from him. Nor was there much to be gained by bringing Phil up on more serious charges. What he had tried to do to me would be the stuff of my dreams for some time, but I really didn't want him to languish for decades in prison. He'd been nice to me in his way, until he wasn't.

"So what do you say, Ms. Revere, are you still on board with us?" Mr. Kerr asked. I could see he was concerned, by the furrowing of his brow. If I refused, things could get pretty sticky for them.

I stood up and put out my hand. "Thank you for the promotion, sir."

"Congratulations," he said with a smile of relief. "And I hope this is the start of a long and successful relationship."

I walked downstairs and through the lobby still feeling a bit stunned. I wasn't quite happy enough to celebrate. Getting the position of associate fair and square would have been better than receiving it as part of a complex deal to save the firm's image. But rarely do things work out perfectly in such an imperfect world.

Chapter 20

I walked up the stairs to my apartment, anxious to tell someone about my promotion. There really wasn't anyone to tell but Cindy, so I knocked on her door. She answered the door half dressed.

"Sorry, Madison, I can't have dinner with you tonight. Myles is coming over to take me out. I was late getting home because I had to do three perms this afternoon."

I felt so frustrated that I wanted to cry, not an emotion I frequently indulge in.

"I just wanted to tell you that I got an important promotion at work today."

She stopped and gave me a quick hug. "That's wonderful, honey; you'll have to tell me all about it tomorrow."

I felt an over whelming desire to say something—anything—to get her to stand still and really pay attention to me the way Mother never did.

"I also wanted to tell you that Otto saved my life last night, so you should really give him something extra special to eat."

"Sure," she said only half-aware of what I had said. Suddenly, it clicked. "Did you say that Otto saved your life?" She stood still and her eyes opened wide.

"I nodded. I took him to the office last night because I had a meeting with a man I worked with, and I didn't want to leave Otto alone. The man tried to kill me, and Otto saved my life. He was very brave."

"You took my dog with you to meet a killer," she said, the outrage growing in her voice.

"No. I didn't know the man was a killer. He had some kind of a breakdown and went berserk," I said, presenting the firm's colorful story. "Otto stopped the man when he tried to kill me, and I was able to subdue my attacker."

I could see Cindy trying to decide whether to believe me or not. Finally, because she knows I never lie, she came over and gave me a long hug. "Are you all right? Were you hurt?"

"I'm fine. Thanks to Otto."

Cindy gave Otto an admiring glance. Otto stared back as if he knew we were talking about him. "Yes," Cindy said. "He really is better than any man."

After a few more words with Cindy about the relative merits of the male canine compared to the male human, I went into my apartment. I felt like I should open a bottle of champagne because that's what people do on special occasions. But I didn't have any, and the occasion was rapidly starting to feel something less than special. I had changed my clothes and popped a diet entrée into the microwave when the phone rang. It was my sister Janice.

"How are you, Madison?" she asked.

I was about to tell her about my promotion, and maybe even share the truth about what had happened at Baker, Kerr, and Finch, when she interrupted me.

"Dad is staying with me," she announced.

"How nice of him to help you with the children now that you're alone."

"Actually, he's pretty helpful, but that's not why he's here. Mother threw him out."

"Why?"

"Well, apparently ten years ago Dad did have a short fling with a woman working for another firm whose books Dad checked."

That was an interesting expression for it, I thought.

"And Mother's private detective was very thorough. Apparently this woman has since found religion, and she was happy to confess her earlier indiscretion. Once Mother heard about it she threw Dad out."

"How is he taking it?" I asked.

"Surprisingly well. Actually, he seems like a new man. Suddenly he's become a really fascinating guy, talking about all sorts of things that I never knew he was interested in; things that he didn't talk about in front of Mother because she didn't want to hear about them. I'm afraid Dad was really into self-censorship. Now he acts like a man suddenly free to be himself."

"But what about Mother? She must be devastated."

"She's very hard to reach. Apparently within a matter of twelve hours after throwing Dad out, she joined a group for separated and divorced women. The one time I spoke with her, she was very much into organizing the group to be more radically activist. It seems to me that she's directing all of the energy she used to put into organizing our family into mobilizing this group."

"If that's true, by the end of the week they should be changing the world."

Janice laughed. "One positive result is that she is now convinced that throwing Peter out was one of the best things I've ever done in my life."

"Nothing like walking in the other person's shoes for a few hours to change the perspective. Would it be possible to talk with Dad?"

"He's upstairs reading a bedtime story to the girls right now. Also, he's quite embarrassed about his little fling. He found it hard to talk about with me, and I think he's going to need a little time before he can discuss it with you and Adam."

"I understand. Well, tell him I support him in whatever he decides to do from now on, and he can give me a call whenever he's ready. I suppose I should call Mother sometime."

"There's no rush; she's so busy."

"I wanted to tell her that I got promoted to associate."

"That's great! Congratulations! By all means tell her, but don't expect it to make much impact on her anymore. You could be appointed to the Supreme Court, and I doubt it would make a dent, unless you were going to improve the rights of women. Family is no longer the center of her life. The sisterhood is."

We chatted for a few minutes more. I sat there musing over my mother, the neo-feminist. I was sure she'd be just as overbearing in that role, but I hoped that perhaps we'd have more in common.

I pulled my dried out entrée from the microwave and ate it with a glass of wine from a bottle I'd opened some time in the distant past. Not much of a celebration, but I was feeling pretty content with it.

Whether it was the wine or the excitement of the day, by the time I got done eating, I was barely able to clean up and change into my pajamas. When my head hit the pillow, I fell into a deep sleep.

Chapter 21

When I got into the office, Sherri was already there, sitting at her desk and staring into space. She actually gave me a friendly good morning, no doubt happy to see at least someone she knew. I didn't know whether she was going to be shifted into Mr. Kerr's secretarial pool now that Finch was gone or whether she would be let go. I had a suspicion that she didn't know yet either. She had been with Finch for so long, she could easily be lumped in with him and fired. Although there had never been any love lost between us, she was an efficient secretary and deserved better.

Thinking she probably needed some sense of continuity, I made the morning coffee. She might want a cup, and I knew that I would.

I spent the next hour printing out my report on the Mercer estate. I knew no eyes other than Mr. Kerr's would ever see it, unless Baker had some interest, but I wanted him to be aware of the amount of effort I had put into it. When it was complete and well secured in an envelope, I took it next door and gave it to Mr. Kerr's secretary.

I spotted Reggie going into her office. I went over and said hello. She motioned me into her office and shut the door.

"So they finally got rid of Finch? I told you they would eventually. His public behavior was dragging down the firm. Do you have any idea what was the final straw?"

I shook my head. "It's all been kind of hush-hush."

"Yeah. And where is Phil these days? I haven't seen him around."

"He's had some emotional problems, and decided to leave the firm for treatment."

"What a shame! I really liked him. He was such a normal guy for a lawyer."

I agreed. Someday I'd be able to say more positive things about Phil, but not just yet.

"And stupid me," said Reggie, "I should have started off by congratulating you on your promotion to associate." She gave me a hug. "No one deserves it more."

"Thanks. And you know, I've been thinking. Now that the pressure of getting promoted is off, I'd like to take you up on your offer of letting me train with you for that November marathon."

"Sounds great."

"When and how much do you train?" I asked.

"Three mornings a week, I get up at five and run six miles. On Saturday I do twelve and take Sunday off. I'll have to up my miles on weekends soon. It's getting close to the race."

"It must be pretty dark at five in the morning," I said with a shiver.

Reggie smiled. "It definitely makes a woman of you."

"Well, count me in. I'll give it a try," I said, figuring that if my mother could attempt something new, so could I.

A few minutes later, I was back behind my desk staring out toward the ocean. I had a few odds and ends of projects I'd put off while working on the Mercer file to occupy myself, but by tomorrow I'd have to talk to Kerr about what I should take on next. Hopefully, I'd be getting more interesting work now that I was an associate.

I heard someone clear his throat behind me, and I spun my chair around. Officer Parker stood in the doorway, but he wasn't in uniform. He wore a polo shirt and jeans. Civilian clothes made him look younger, and I admired the way his shirt accentuated his deep chest and broad shoulders.

"May I come in?" he asked.

I nodded toward the chair in front of my desk, and he settled into it.

"I would have come by yesterday to see how you were doing, but things got hectic. How are you?" He stared hard at me, so I knew it was a serious question.

"I think I'm doing okay. Some of it may come back to haunt me, but so far so good."

"I'm sorry we couldn't get Phil on more serious charges. Things happened above my pay grade."

"It's all been explained to me. Phil was my friend up until he tried to kill me, so I'm not feeling very vindictive. But if it hadn't been for Otto and that blackjack you gave me, things could easily have turned out differently. Thank you."

Parker smiled. "Sorry we had to take it into evidence. I'll get you another one right away."

"I'd appreciate it. I seem to be using it a lot lately. One good thing did happen. I got promoted."

"Congratulations. Did you spend last night celebrating?"

I shook my head. "No one to celebrate with."

"We could remedy that tonight if you'd like to go out with me."

I smiled. "I'd like that a lot, as long as we don't go to the Shore Side Inn. I've been attacked the last two times I went there."

"Then the third time is the charm. And I promise that if you get attacked again, I'll do a better job than your friend Eric at protecting you."

"Fair enough, Officer Parker. But I can't really go on calling you Officer Parker, can I?"

"Parker would be fine."

"You don't have a first name?"

"It's Jerome. I'd prefer to forget it."

"Agreed."

"What should I call you?"

"Madison—never Maddy."

"Agreed."

We smiled at each other, and I definitely felt that my life had taken a turn for the better.

THE END

ABOUT THE AUTHOR

Glen Ebisch is also the author of the Pastor Clarissa Abbot Mystery series for Cozy Cat Press which includes *Seaside Secrets* and *Ocean Blues*. Also published by Cozy Cat Press is his mystery *The Black Dog*, in the Marcie and Amanda series.

A retired professor of philosophy, Ebisch has had over 30 mysteries published. He currently resides in western Massachusetts. Feel free to contact him at his website www.glenebisch.com. If you enjoyed this book, a review on Amazon would be appreciated.

Made in the USA
Columbia, SC
14 September 2023

22852241R00102